KISS OF A DUKE

ERICA RIDLEY

♡ Erica Ridley

ISBN: 1943794537
ISBN-13: 978-1943794539
Copyright © 2018 Erica Ridley
Model Photography © PeriodImages
Cover Design © Teresa Spreckelmeyer

ALSO BY ERICA RIDLEY

Rogues to Riches:

Lord of Chance

Lord of Pleasure

Lord of Night

Lord of Temptation

Lord of Secrets

Lord of Vice

Dukes of War:

The Viscount's Tempting Minx

The Earl's Defiant Wallflower

The Captain's Bluestocking Mistress

The Major's Faux Fiancée

The Brigadier's Runaway Bride

The Pirate's Tempting Stowaway

The Duke's Accidental Wife

The 12 Dukes of Christmas:

Once Upon a Duke

Kiss of a Duke

Wish Upon a Duke

Never Say Duke

Dukes, Actually

Welcome to Christmas!

Our picturesque village is nestled around Marlowe Castle, high atop the gorgeous mountain we call home. Cressmouth is best known for our year-round Yuletide cheer. Here, we're family.

The legend of our twelve dukes? Absolutely true! But perhaps not always in the way one might expect…

CHAPTER 1

Marlowe Castle
Christmas, England

"*T*o the *Duke!*" yelled a half-sotted voice in the middle of the packed ballroom.

"To Penelope Mitchell!" the crowd shouted back, raising their goblets of spiced wine in unison.

Clinks of crystal glasses and peals of merry laughter filled the high-ceilinged assembly room as the spectators' cheers warmed the nutmeg-scented air.

Despite this being the third such toast in the past half hour, Miss Penelope Mitchell still couldn't quite credit that the entirety of her mountaintop village had crowded into the castle's largest chamber to celebrate something other than the year-round Christmastide their town was primarily known for.

As a lady chemist, she couldn't be prouder.

Her satisfaction wasn't solely because the townsfolk had gathered to celebrate the accomplishments of a woman, or even because the accomplishment in question was a perfume she had invented herself.

As far as Penelope was concerned, she and one thousand of her neighbors had gathered to celebrate a breakthrough in *science*.

Unlike more well-known natural philosophers, Penelope's primary field of study was neither plant life nor the animal kingdom. The majority of her observations and chemical experiments took place in the custom-built laboratory next to her kitchen. An unobtrusive metal firewall separated both rooms from the rest of the house in case of accidental fire or explosion.

Today, it was Penelope's soaring heart that felt close to detonation.

"Congratulations!" shouted her bosom friend Miss Gloria Godwin over the joyous din of the crowd.

Although Gloria directed her passions toward the infinite expanse of the heavens whilst Penelope preferred to focus on glass vials of chemicals she could hold in her hands, the two had been inseparable since childhood.

"Thank you," Penelope said, as soon as she edged close enough not to have to shout. The party had been underway less than an hour, and already she feared losing her voice before morning. "I cannot believe *Duke* is this successful."

"It isn't," Gloria said matter-of-factly. "The party isn't for your perfume. The celebration is for *you*. We're proud all of England has recognized your talent."

Penelope gave her a crooked grin. "Who knew our town's resident lady chemist would become a champion not only of science, but of fashion?"

"I did," Gloria said without hesitation.

Penelope's cheeks heated. "You're a good friend."

"And you're mad as a hatter," Gloria replied with a flash of her dimples. "But it seems so is everyone else. There's nothing England likes better than to copy whatever barmy antics appear in the scandal sheets. I ask you, what sort of man would douse himself with animal secretions in an attempt to attract a woman?"

"A wise man who understands science," Penelope protested. "It's chemistry, not madness. A natural reaction. When the olfactory glands of certain mammals are exposed to the—"

"Stop right there." Gloria covered her ears and pretended not to hear. "This is a party, not the annual gathering of the Natural Philosophers Society." She frowned. "*Is* there a Natural Philosophers Society?"

Penelope opened her mouth to answer.

"No, don't tell me. Don't tell anyone," Gloria said quickly. "That's not why we're here, darling. No one cares *how* your perfume works. They just love that it *does*. All those articles and caricatures and gossip columns with stories of previously unrakish men being practically trampled by eligible females within minutes of applying your *eau de toilette*… You're a genius."

Penelope swallowed an uncomfortable lump in her throat at the praise. "It's not genius. Experiment after experiment has proven that the properly proportioned secretions of both musk whales and civets—"

"No, no, no." Gloria grabbed a fresh glass of mulled wine from a passing footman and shoved it into Penelope's hands. "Do *not* explain how it works. To anyone. That ruins the magic."

With a sigh of frustration, Penelope lowered her nose to smell the steam of her spiced wine. Of course "how it works" was the important bit. Chemists, natural philosophers, and alchemists alike dedicated their lives to trying to decipher the workings of nature. Being able to turn an undesirable element into a desirable one was the entire point.

"Then what *is* the 'magic?'" she asked.

Gloria raised her brows in surprise. "*Prinney* wears your perfume, because none other than Beau Brummell told him true gentlemen shan't leave their dressing rooms without it. The Prince Regent! In your perfume! *That's* the magic. Now that you're famous—"

"I'm not famous," Penelope reminded her. "A specific combination of painstakingly researched olfactory elements is famous."

"—our town is more renowned, too," Gloria continued, brown eyes shining. "I shouldn't be surprised if we have twice as many visitors this year, from those wishing to see the birthplace of *Duke*."

"My laboratory?" Penelope reared back in horror. "I allow no one inside. In order to keep the pristine environment unadulterated with—"

"Not your laboratory," Gloria assured her. "They want to see the beautiful Christmas village that inspires you. Who wouldn't want to visit a snow-topped mountain and return home inspired, too?"

Penelope tightened her lips, lest the truth spill out. She wasn't inspired by a snow-dusted mountaintop village, no matter how picturesque. She was driven by molecules and vials and complex chemical compositions. The irony was remarkable.

She hadn't intended to turn London's fashionable set on their ears. She had been competing in a nationwide quest to determine causal factors in the mating habits of certain nocturnal mammals. Her intent had been to prove that lady natural philosophers were just as competent at investigation as their male counterparts.

That her research should result in the discovery of a chemical compound just as potent when applied to humans had been incidental to her cause. When she'd packaged it as *Duke* and sold it on a lark, she hadn't anticipated how quickly the new scent would take over local shops, then regional distributors, then national magazines, then end up as part of the morning toilette of the most influential man in England.

Or that Brummel would convince Prinney, too.

She grinned at Gloria. Progress had been made. The Natural Philosophers Guild had refused to allow a lady chemist's research into their precious contest, but England had taken notice nonetheless. What did it matter that their fellow villagers had come to celebrate scents rather than science? Her smile dipped.

"Where's Penelope?" boomed a voice from across the tumultuous chamber.

"Speech!" shouted another.

Penelope ducked her head to hide her face before she could be spotted. She was used to spending weeks at a time in the privacy of her laboratory. Not pontificating on stage in front of her neighbors. If she stayed near the back, they wouldn't find her.

"Speech, speech!" the crowd echoed in raptures.

"Go on, you brilliant woman." Gloria tried to nudge her in the direction of the grand dais on the other side of the ballroom. "Your people await."

Penelope sent a dubious glance in the direction of the dais. She couldn't even see it behind all the people. "What do they expect me to say?"

"You gave them what we all want," Gloria explained with a smile. "A tool to help them find love. What could be purer?"

"That's not what I did at all," Penelope said in surprise.

"Speech, speech!" cried the crowd.

"I didn't say you personally acted as matchmaker," Gloria chided her gently. "But you created a perfume that enables two previously unknown people to come together and perhaps discover love."

"I created a chemical solution that enabled two previously unconnected *compounds* to come together," Penelope stammered. "It has nothing to do with love."

"Everything has to do with love," Gloria said.

Penelope shook her head. "There is no love. It's an illusion. A romantic fantasy invented to explain chemical reactions as old as nature itself."

Gloria's mouth fell open. "How can you say that? You camped in tents for months and witnessed the effects of your compounds firsthand. If your perfumes can make rodents fall in love, you cannot deny that—"

"Civets are Viverridae, more similar to primitive felines than rodents," Penelope interrupted. "And they don't *fall in love*. Their females go *in heat*. In fact, as Samuel Williams wrote in his *Natural and Civil History of Vermont—*"

"What do American natural philosophers know about love?" Gloria spluttered.

"That it doesn't exist," Penelope blurted out.

"Speech, speech!" screamed the crowd.

"Love is a fictional construct invented to make natural biological urges sound more palatable in Polite Society," Penelope explained earnestly. "Animals excrete scents. Humans are animals. If we're in love with anything, it's our own excretions."

"Good God." Gloria stared at her in disbelief. "That is the least romantic—"

"Romance is an arbitrarily prescribed set of unnatural behaviors and absurd superstitions created to explain and engender a mythical emotion we invented whole cloth. All because we believe ourselves to be superior to other animals."

Gloria spluttered in disbelief. "Surely you agree modern society is superior to the lives of rodents and primitive cats!"

Penelope sniffed. "Male civets don't douse themselves with the glandular excretions of other, more popular civets in order to attract the attention of voluptuous female civets at local assemblies."

"They would if they could," Gloria muttered beneath her breath. "All males are optimists."

"Speech, speech!" roared the crowd.

"Someone fetch Penelope Mitchell!" shouted a man near the dais.

"I see her!" a woman shrieked. "She's with Miss Godwin!"

Penelope rolled back her shoulders. "Very well. I don't know anything about love—"

"*Obviously*," Gloria muttered, louder this time.

"—but science has proven that olfactory information can incite sexual arousal in both genders of many animals, causing the mating instinct to demand immediate and natural carnal satisfaction. I can talk about that. I've personally observed many instances of—"

Gloria grabbed Penelope's arm and turned her away from the stage.

"No speech!" she shouted over her shoulder. "Miss Mitchell is much too shy and... er... ladylike. She appreciates your support. Enjoy the party! And the wine! Talk amongst yourselves!"

"Furthermore," Penelope continued thoughtfully as her best friend tugged her a safer distance from the dais, "I'm *glad* I'm in no danger of 'falling in love.' I like being a chemist and I like being a spinster. There's no reason to fuss with the permanency of a husband if all a woman wishes to do is satisfy the occasional natural urge."

Gloria wrinkled her nose. "But what about all the other women?"

Penelope tilted her head. "What other women?"

"The ladies who *do* wish to fuss with the permanency of a husband. You might not have a biological or financial or romantical need for marriage, but I daresay most women do not have that luxury. They *have* to marry." Gloria's voice faltered. "And we like to believe in love."

Penelope's heart twisted in remorse. Gloria was right. Penelope might be too rational for romance, but that was no reason to ruin the experience for anyone else. In fact, Penelope was in a unique position to actually do something about it.

"You've inspired me," she announced.

"I-I've inspired you?" Gloria stammered in obvious concern. "To do what?"

"To help," Penelope said. She gave a sharp nod.

Gloria blinked. "Help how?"

"With science." Penelope tapped her chin. "What did *Duke* do?"

"Make an obscene amount of money?" Gloria guessed. "Revolutionize modern perfumes?"

"*Men's* perfumes," Penelope corrected with chagrin. "An easy market, and a mistake. The world doesn't need more dandies and rakes."

"What does it need?" Gloria asked suspiciously.

"Empowered women," Penelope replied without hesitation. "I cannot control Society, but I *do* control what I research in my laboratory. *Duke* was just the beginning. I have more research. The next product I launch will be *Duchess*." She straightened her shoulders in determination. "For women."

Gloria clasped her hands to her chest. "You could make a perfume to help women find husbands?"

Penelope nodded. "Or become female rakes.

Ladies' choice. Once you attract a man, it's up to you if you want to keep him."

Gloria burst out laughing. "There's no such thing as lady rakes."

"There should be." Penelope gave her a wicked grin. "Why should men have all the fun?"

"Speaking of rakes…" Gloria grabbed Penelope's arm and bounced on her toes. "Don't look now, but Nicholas Pringle just walked into the ballroom. Nicholas Pringle! Here, in this very ballroom."

Penelope shrugged. "Who?"

"Only the most fawned-over rake to ever grace the Society pages. I recognize him from the caricatures alone. He once—Is that his *brother*?" Gloria let out an appreciative whistle beneath her breath. "It must be a brother. He looks just like him. Don't look! They'll know we're talking about them. My heart is pounding. I can't believe this is happening."

"I can't believe you're overreacting." Penelope gave an exaggerated yawn. "How handsome can two men be?"

"I'm not overreacting," Gloria promised. "I'm just the first to—"

Audible female gasps rippled through the crowd, followed by several dramatic swoons.

"—the first to notice," Gloria finished smugly. "They call him 'Saint Nick' because he's as wicked as they come. One look and you're smitten."

Penelope raised a brow.

Gloria fluttered her eyelashes. "At least I didn't swoon."

"No, but you bruised my arm." Penelope wrenched out of Gloria's grasp and angled her head toward the open ballroom doors. "Where are they?"

Gloria fanned her throat. "Saint Nick is the gentleman with—"

"Found him." The strangled words barely escaped Penelope's suddenly dry throat. Gloria was right.

From a biological perspective, he was the finest male specimen Penelope had ever seen. And as a living, breathing woman... Good heavens.

Features: symmetrical. Jawline: chiseled. Visage: arresting. Light brown hair tumbled over a perfectly shaped head. His cravat was as white as chemists' talcum, a subtle explosion of sharp points and soft folds designed to add elegance without distracting from the rest of the package.

And Saint Nick made one tempting package.

The hard curves of his muscled arms and wide shoulders were shown to advantage in a dashing coat of black superfine that begged to be touched. His waistcoat was the shimmery silver of magnesium, an element oft-combined with iron. She wondered if his will was just as strong.

Coal-black boots, tight-fitting buckskins, kid gloves... All he'd need to do was jingle a bell and every woman present would clamor to be his.

Every woman but Penelope.

Yes, his looks were the very definition of all that was virile and desirable in a gentleman. But his approach to life made him the last man who could hold her interest. He was an accomplished rake. A man who relied on *romance* to woo silly women.

The urge to spread one's seed might be a natural male directive, but Penelope would never fawn over a man with nothing to recommend him beyond symmetrical features and pretty words. She had better things to do. Her mind preferred the comfort and excitement of her laboratory to pointless strolls down moonlit paths with a man who couldn't hold a meaningful conversation.

Penelope cared about facts, about science, about logic. A natural philosopher would never select a mating partner based on external beauty alone.

"Uninterested," she said abruptly. "Shall we find the dessert buffet?"

"We should find someone to introduce us," Gloria breathed. "I had no idea Saint Nick had a younger brother. I'm very, very interested."

Penelope frowned. "If you had no idea he existed, how do you know he's the younger brother?"

"Because Nicholas Pringle is first in line to a dukedom," Gloria replied with a cheeky grin. "Scoff at Society papers all you like. Some of us use them for important research."

Penelope gave an affectionate roll of her eyes. "I wouldn't want a husband who must mind a dukedom."

"Low probability," Gloria answered promptly. "He's heir presumptive to the Duke of Silkridge, whose first banns were announced last Sunday. The Pringle brothers are his cousins. They've no other titles, which means they visit London for social reasons, rather than to attend the House of Lords. I presume their country piles are elsewhere."

Penelope burst out laughing. "You *have* done a lot of research."

Gloria gave an angelic smile. "What else am I to do? Spinsters like me have to wait around for your new perfume in order to have a chance. Unless opportunity knocks. Let's go introduce ourselves to the Pringle brothers."

"Absolutely not."

Gloria's brows arched in surprise. "Because Saint Nick is a rake? Since when do you care about propriety?"

Penelope shook her head. "Because you're right. I should be working on the new perfume. I started a female version at the same time as the male version, but *Duke* was easier. I halted the other project when I learned the Natural Philosophers Guild was seeking applicants to research practical applications of John Dalton's atomic theory."

Gloria's mouth fell open. "You mean... it's almost done and you abandoned it? The magical *eau de toilette* that could have viscounts and earls swooning at my feet?"

"It's close," Penelope hedged. "I'm not yet in a position to declare with empirical certainty that *Duchess* will outperform *Duke*, but I intend to lock myself in my laboratory until it's ready for trials."

"All the more reason to introduce ourselves to the Pringle brothers while they're still here." Gloria narrowed her eyes. "A month from now, after I bathe myself in reptile excretions —or whatever ungodly concoction you plan to create—when I next meet him in a crowded ballroom, I can say, 'Why, Mr. Pringle, I haven't seen you since the Christmas soirée!' And he'll say, 'Mmrrgle blrrrgmmph' as he falls at my feet in a manly, yet glorious, swoon."

Penelope shook her finger in mock reprimand. "If you apply more than the recommended dosage, *all* the men in the ballroom will say 'Mmrrgle blrrrgmmph' in unison as they crumple gracelessly to your feet."

"Even better," Gloria said with delight. "Nothing starts a conversation quite like regaining consciousness among a dizzy heap of equally smitten gentlemen."

"Once the new perfume is ready, women needn't bother *talking* to prospective gentlemen anymore," Penelope promised. "Chemistry will take over and the subsequent natural urges will guide them straight into your arms."

Gloria pushed her lips into a pout. "What about those of us who *enjoy* talking to men?"

"Ninnies, all of you." Penelope linked her arm with Gloria's. "I'd rather hold a conversation with a *bain marie* than some empty-headed rake."

"Even one as wicked and handsome as Saint Nick?"

"Especially not him," Penelope replied firmly. "Now, where was that dessert buffet?"

CHAPTER 2

*M*r. Nicholas Pringle came to an abrupt halt inside the doorway of an enormous ballroom. He had no choice. The extravagant, high-vaulted chamber was packed elbow-to-elbow with what appeared to be every resident—and guest—of the small mountaintop village known as Christmas.

Ladies in fine frocks and gentlemen in tailored waistcoats. Ordinary men and women who looked as though they'd strolled into the castle straight from their farm, shop, or garden. A fair number of children not yet old enough to be presented at court squeezed through the bustling crowd to pilfer treats from an extensive buffet that an army of cooks would struggle to keep replenished.

Nicholas turned to his brother in disbelief. "This is your idea of a small, intimate gathering to get to know our temporary neighbors?"

Chris tossed him an unrepentant grin. "It's even better than I had hoped."

"What did you hope?" Nicholas asked suspiciously.

"The posted bills invited townsfolk to celebrate the success of a local perfumer," his brother admitted. "I didn't mention the details because it sounded…"

"Boring?" Nicholas put in dryly.

"As you can see, it is not! We are in luck." Chris's brow creased. "That is, if we can edge ourselves inside the ballroom."

"Allow me," Nicholas said magnanimously and rose to his full height in order to cast a practiced smile at the ladies most likely to recognize him.

His brother reached for his arm. "No! Don't—"

It was too late. The curve of Nicholas's "sensuous mouth" (as reported by the scandal columns) and the glint of wicked promise in his "sapphire irises" (never described as mere cerulean) had already wrought their magic.

A river of breathless gasps rippled through the female portion of the crowd, in many cases accompanied by the clutch of dainty hands to suddenly heaving breasts or the flurry of a painted fan aimed at an overheated décolletage.

"Six," Chris said in disgust. "One half-smile from you and half a dozen perfectly healthy ladies swoon to their feet."

"Nonsense. This crush is packed far too

dense for anyone to fall down." Nicholas yanked his brother forward. "You go first. They're making way."

After the briefest of baleful glares, his brother led the way deeper into the crowd.

Nicholas allowed himself a small grin. He and his brother were both here for the same reason: women. But there the similarity ended.

Chris sought a gentle young lady of good breeding and pretty manners with whom he could fall in love and marry. Together they would fill a large nursery with spoiled, happy children.

Nicholas could not imagine a worse fate. His tastes ran to women who preferred a quick tumble over boring talk. Those who measured their liaisons in hours, not lifetimes.

His recent fame in the caricatures had only deepened his rakish reputation. The women who chased him sought conquest, not courtship. Nicholas didn't mind. The last thing he needed was to entangle himself with a marriageable woman. He would gladly hand all of those to his brother.

"Speech, speech!" came a shout from the other side of the ballroom.

The crowd roared its agreement.

"Are you certain this party is about perfume?" Nicholas asked. "What can possibly be said about toilet water that we don't already know?"

"This is the birthplace of *Duke*," his brother

answered with reverence. "The inventor is somewhere in this room."

A flood of irritation washed away Nicholas's buoyant good humor.

"Where?" He curled his hands into fists. "I'll throttle the cretin right now."

"It'll ruin your image," Christopher chided him. "And mine. No throttling."

"That horrid perfume is a plague upon London," Nicholas growled. "It's ruining my life."

"I like how it smells." Chris shrugged. "So does everyone else."

Nicholas scowled at him. "That's what's horrid about it."

"That it works?"

"Yes." Nicholas said with feeling. "It shouldn't exist. A rake is a noble calling—"

"What's noble about it?" his brother cut in skeptically.

"—in which a man utilizes his mind—"

"His body, you mean." Christopher smirked. "The primary criteria for 'rakedom' seems to be nothing more than a handsome face and a hard—"

"—in order to engage a willing female participant in a few hours of mutual satisfaction." Nicholas narrowed his eyes. "This pox of a perfume has every dandy, greenhorn, and featherwit in London dousing himself in *eau de toilette* and believing himself a dashing conqueror of women."

Chris lifted a shoulder. "The ladies do seem to like it."

"It's cheating," Nicholas said firmly.

"So is having a handsome face," his brother countered. "See how well you do with a flour sack wrapped about your head."

Nicholas sent him a flat stare. "My face is real. This accursed perfume is false. It must be stopped."

"Don't wear it," Chris suggested.

"I would never," Nicholas said in outrage. "One shouldn't need to smell like a duke in order to find a woman."

"I wonder if it smells like any dukes we know," his brother mused.

"It smells like all the dukes we know," Nicholas gritted out. "And the earls and the viscounts and the footmen and the furriers and the bakers and the butchers and the—"

"Everyone's wearing it. I know," Chris interrupted with a grin. "That's the point of this party. *Duke* works. I've heard no less than a dozen gentlemen swear it was their key to securing a bride."

"No man should use a parlor trick to attract women," Nicholas snapped. "Whether it's to take them to bed or to the altar. Deception is dishonorable."

"I concede the point," his brother said after a moment's thought. "I would never wed a woman whose interest in me was anything other than genuine. But we have different goals. You are not interested in marriage. Or have things changed?"

"*Never.*"

A chill slid down Nicholas's spine at the very idea. It wasn't just the thought of forever that gave him pause. Wives were alarmingly unpredictable. He preferred knowing exactly what each day would bring.

As a rake, the lines were clearly drawn. One night. One time. Nothing more. Everyone knew what to expect. The women he dallied with sought the same things. They lived in the same world, comported themselves by the same rules. Courtesans, widows, women of independent means who either did not have a reputation to protect or were well-practiced in secrecy.

Nicholas was here for a holiday. This northern village of eternal Christmastide had already given more gifts than anticipated. His brother was welcome to woo any doe-eyed virgin or proper young lady he might wish. The fallen women were the only ones Nicholas was interested in. They wanted a good time; he could provide it.

Chris glanced over his shoulder as if hearing his thoughts. "Aren't you getting a little too old to pursue the life of a rake?"

"How old is too old for pleasure?" Nicholas countered. A preposterous notion. What else was the point of life?

"At least admit we are getting too old for debutantes," his brother insisted.

"I've never wanted one," Nicholas said with a shiver. Ghastly thought.

"What *do* you want?" his brother asked softly. "Do you know?"

Nicholas considered the question. At six-and-thirty, he much preferred ladies close to his age.

Over the years, he had been propositioned by every kind. Married, widowed, fallen. They weren't after romance, but distraction. Nicholas was happy to provide it. None of them were looking for love. It wasn't a service he provided, or even a concept he believed in.

His brother, on the other hand... Nicholas arched his brows. "I suppose you believe your future bride is elbowing her way through this crush, guided by Fate itself into your open, willing arms?"

"I hope so," Chris said fervently. "Isn't that what we all want?"

Nicholas stared at him. "I cannot imagine wanting to wake up to the same woman day after day."

Nor would they wish that with him. For ladies seeking husbands, he was a terrible choice. For those seeking one night of pleasure, however... He was exactly the right man.

His brother leaned forward earnestly. "Haven't you ever had an evening so perfect that you wished every day going forward would be just like it?"

"Not once."

Nicholas didn't even have to think it over. He had never even wished to spend a week with the same woman.

"There she is!" His brother tilted his head excitedly in the approximate direction of three hundred celebrating villagers.

"There who is?" Nicholas craned his neck. "Your future bride?"

"The inventor of *Duke*." Chris explained, his eyes shining. "The reason everyone's here."

"Wait. The evil perfumer turning every idiot in London into a self-professed rake is a woman?" Nicholas said in disbelief.

Chris raised his brows. "Are you interested now?"

"Very interested," Nicholas replied. But not for the reason his brother expected.

He wanted a private audience with the lady perfumer for something else entirely.

CHAPTER 3

*N*icholas hid the flower he'd purchased from the castle greenhouse behind his back and turned up the snow-dusted walk leading to the perfumer's front door. No matter how hard he tried, life was full of surprises.

Instead of visiting comely ladies of ill repute, today's target was some bluestocking lady chemist whose naïve oversight had spawned chaos in London's previously stable social order. The only way to stem the explosion of faux rakelings was to halt production of *Duke*.

At least the errand should only take a moment. Not because Nicholas expected his reputation to do the work. By all accounts, Miss Mitchell was as awkward and science-obsessed and reclusive as the most fervent of her male counterparts. The lady was unlikely to have heard of him.

In this case, one could not count on so-called sapphire irises or the curve of his smile to sway her. The rose in his hand was just for insurance. Nicholas intended to appeal to her logic. As a natural philosopher, she was no doubt already immersed in some new project. He would encourage her to give up *Duke* and focus on that instead.

His knock upon the door was answered by neither a maid nor a butler, but the lady chemist herself. Miss Mitchell wore thick leather mitts with strange burn marks, a stiff gray smock dusted in white powder, and a beleaguered expression. "What?"

Nicholas thrust the flower forward out of reflex.

The prevailing wisdom was that roses could dissolve any disagreement between a lady and a gentleman. Because he had never returned for a second day's company with the same woman, Nicholas had never had to test the theory. He hoped his brother was right.

It did not appear so.

Rather than coo or simper or whatever female reaction single red roses were meant to elicit, Miss Mitchell glanced over her shoulder as if she had left something far more interesting in another room before returning her irritated gaze to Nicholas. "Did you want something?"

What was the best opening gambit?

Her eyes were neither cobalt nor emerald

nor turquoise, but brown: a color rarely waxed poetic upon by romantic fools. Clearly, they had never glimpsed Miss Mitchell's eyes. Hers were not a dull brown, or a forgettable brown, or even a plain, serviceable brown. Not even the brown of coffee or cinnamon or chocolate.

Hers were different from all the other brown eyes Nicholas had ever seen. Deeper. Sharper. More dangerous. These were eyes that did not merely look, but *saw*. He would need to be careful.

"Forgive me for not waiting for a formal introduction," he said pleasantly, lifting the perfect rose a little higher so she could not miss it. "My name is—"

"'Saint Nick', the infamous London rake." She pursed her lips. "I've heard."

Well. That explained the frosty welcome.

"My calling card phrases it a bit differently," he said, and tried again. "I am Mr. Nicholas Pringle of London, and I am pleased to make your acquaintance."

"That makes one of us." She sent another impatient glance over her shoulder. "I'm not interested in you or your services. Is that all?"

"I'm not offering myself to you," Nicholas stammered. There was nothing to purchase. He wasn't a cicisbeo. Good God. How had he lost control of what was meant to be an easy conversation? "I was merely hoping for a brief tête-à-tête."

She arched a brow. "Then why bring a flower?"

Excellent point, blast it. He'd known her eyes would see too much. He chucked the rose onto a snow bank. "Now may I come inside?"

A sudden, deafening din rent the air like the chaos of a hundred woodpeckers drilling their beaks in unison against a sea of clattering pots.

"Very well," Miss Mitchell said and disappeared.

At least, Nicholas presumed she'd said *very well* aloud. He could hear nothing over the ungodly racket. The last thing he wanted to do was inch closer to it.

He stepped over the threshold anyway. If he came back some other time, the chemist might not allow him inside. This was his chance. The perfect, golden opportunity to... to... Good God, how could anyone think with that brain-splitting clamor rattling the walls?

"Miss Mitchell?" he shouted. Or hoped he shouted. He could not hear himself over the infernal noise. "Do you need help with—"

All sound abruptly stopped. A heavy silence filled the air so thick and so absolute it was almost more deafening than the cacophony had been.

His ears felt as though they were underwater. He couldn't hear anything. Not the wind, not the ticking of a clock, not the noise from the street outside. Only the sound of his own startled intake of breath assured him he hadn't been struck deaf.

Miss Mitchell appeared from around the corner, wiping a fresh dusting of white powder from her smock as if nothing of interest had occurred. "You were saying?"

Nicholas cleared his throat. "Might I ask the origin of that fascinating sound?"

"My kitchen alarm," she said with all the same import one might give a comment upon the weather. "When I reinforced the walls to inhibit distribution of sound, I had to counteract my own efforts by inventing an alarm with even greater capabilities in order to discern its call when the sound barriers are engaged."

The explanation engendered a dozen new questions. Why had she felt the need to cut off all sound? How had she achieved it? Why create the world's most deafening alarm instead of leaving her door ajar? And most importantly—

"What are you cooking?" he asked.

"Baking," she said. "My maid does the cooking. Baking is chemistry. I never pass up an opportunity for chemistry."

Nicholas hesitated. From any other woman, a rake could correctly assume any oblique comment referencing "chemistry" to be an invitation to create some... all night long.

He was used to women coming to him entranced by tales of his prowess in a bedchamber. Sexual desire was something he understood, something he appreciated, something he enjoyed exploiting with someone who felt the same.

Miss Mitchell clearly was not that woman.

She was singularly unimpressed with his rakish reputation, and thus far remained unswayed by his looks or charm. And yet she had let him in. He straightened. Perhaps she was more open than she seemed.

He gave her a winning smile. "I would like to talk to you about *Duke*."

"You have eight minutes until my biscuits are done."

His stomach immediately growled. "What kind of biscuits?"

She glanced around the corner. "Seven and a half minutes."

"Can we move within sight of the clock?" He flinched. "It won't ring the same alarm again, will it?"

"Yes." Miss Mitchell motioned for him to follow. "This way."

She led him through a thick metal door into the cleanest kitchen he had ever seen.

Although he himself did not bake, as a lad he had learned that befriending the staff of any kitchen was the easiest way to be slipped extra treats. Over the years, he had enjoyed countless jam tartlets, fig pudding, crème brûlée…

But his favorite dessert of all remained fresh-baked biscuits. Crisp on the outside, gooey on the inside. Crumbly and sweet and delicious. Perhaps a sip of cold milk to wash it down.

"Seven minutes," Miss Mitchell said as she hoisted herself on a tall stool near the fire.

He did the same. "I'll cut to the chase. *Duke* is cheating. It must be stopped."

She inclined her head. "Cheating how?"

He considered where to begin. "You accused me of being a rake."

"It was no accusation. You do more than simply dabble in occasional carnal activities. You are an accomplished rake with a well-deserved reputation."

"Exactly." He leaned back. Although the picture she painted wasn't ideal, she had just proven his point. "I deserve my reputation. I earned it through my actions. I did not dump it on from a bottle."

"Yes, the dumping is problematic," she mused. "I am investigating airborne diffusion methods. My theory is that a fine overall mist will prove far superior than concentrated doses applied to limited pulse points."

"You have to stop," he broke in.

She glanced up. "Because you don't think it works?"

"Because it does work. A man shouldn't win a woman because he purchased cologne water."

"Do tell." The corner of Miss Mitchell's mouth twitched. "How *should* a man win a woman?"

Nicholas immediately recognized his mistake.

"No one should win anyone else," he said

quickly. "Love isn't a game. It's something that happens naturally."

By some miracle, lightning did not strike him where he stood.

"*Duke* doesn't promise love," she pointed out with a laugh. "It promises easier access to women."

Nicholas gazed at her in disbelief. Clearly, he had misjudged the situation.

"It delivers on that promise," he agreed carefully. "Therein lies the problem. We should be upholding the standards for love, not lowering female inhibitions."

She arched her brows. "Should we?"

What kind of question was that?

He started over. "You believe in love, don't you?"

"No." She chuckled. "Do you?"

"I… haven't experienced it directly," he hedged. She didn't believe in love?

"But you're searching for it?" she pressed.

"This isn't about me," he said. "I'm not your customer."

She lifted a shoulder. "Then why should I care about your opinion?"

"It's not even *my* opinion," he blurted. "Don't you know other people who believe in love?"

She cocked her head in thought. "Gloria does."

He had no idea who Gloria was, but he was glad the lady believed in fantasies.

"There you have it," he said with relief.

"Gloria believes in love. Don't you think she should find it? What if you discovered her in the arms of the wrong man, all because he hoodwinked her delicate senses with some five-quid manipulative odor?"

Miss Mitchell stared at him. "That is literally the entire reason men are dumping it on by the bucket. They want to be the wrong arms that hapless women tumble into."

"And you wish to be a party to that?" he burst out in disbelief.

"It cannot happen," she said simply. "Women aren't 'hapless.' That is a fiction men choose to believe. Be logical. A manufactured scent may capture a lady's attention, but no perfume melts away clothing. Women make *choices*." She glanced over his shoulder. "Five minutes."

Nicholas ground his jaw. Miss Mitchell was impossible. How could he make her understand? She had thus far been unmoved by appeals to love or emotion. He needed another tack. Which left the most universal motivator of all: money.

He sighed. "I'll buy it from you."

"Five pounds," she said immediately. "You can find a bottle at any chemist's shop."

"No." He leaned forward. "I mean the whole thing. *Duke*. I want full and exclusive rights over production and distribution."

"You want to produce *Duke* yourself?" she asked doubtfully.

Not exactly. He planned to cease production

altogether. Once distribution was up to his discretion, he would simply stop providing it. Situation solved.

He gave her his most charming smile. "Name your price."

CHAPTER 4

*P*enelope gazed beneath her lashes at the dashing London rake seated on one of her worn kitchen stools. As before, she very much saw what all the fuss was about.

The lushly chiseled mouth, the perfectly symmetrical features, the golden stature of tall enough to stand out but not so tall as to make kissing ungainly. With a form like his, anything would look sinful.

Then there was his proposition. Any price she might wish, if she would just sign away all control of the one invention that had ever gained her any recognition whatsoever.

Why had he made the offer? Did he think her driven more by wealth than science? Or perhaps he had been jesting, and had not expected her to consider his proposal for even this long.

She turned to gaze at him directly, giving up any pretense that both he and his proposition were not under intense scrutiny.

No doubt the man was as arrogant as his offer. But there was something more. Something he wasn't telling her. A puzzle.

Although she had known him for less than five minutes, his impassioned criticism of her perfume as an unfair advantage to those who had not earned the privilege had rung true.

Given that perspective, she doubted he had any intention of continuing production of her perfume, were he to gain control of the process. She tilted her head. He had very carefully refrained from false promises. Perhaps due to honor. Or perhaps an old habit from his profession as a rake.

"Is 'rake' a profession?" she asked curiously.

"Are you even thinking about my offer?" he exploded in frustration.

No was on the tip of her tongue, so swift and so sour she could taste it. But she swallowed the urge rather than indulge it. She, too, could be careful with her words. Just because she intended to send him to the devil didn't mean she ought to be hasty in doing so.

"Your objection to *Duke*," she said instead, "is that men who would not otherwise attract certain women are now afforded the same opportunities as accomplished rakes like yourself."

"You see the problem." He gave her an encouraging smile.

She nodded. "I have always seen the problem. I created *Duke* specifically to upset the order you're trying to protect. To give *all* gentlemen the same chance. The shy ones, the bookish ones, the portly ones, the ugly ones, the awkward ones, or anyone else Society deems less worthy. Far from being unjust, *Duke* may be the closest to 'fair' that such gentlemen ever experience."

In fact, it was the reason she began *Duchess*. Women needed every advantage they could get. Particularly overlooked women who deserved to be seen. People like Gloria, who believed in love but lacked dancing partners.

If the right combination of scents afforded an opportunity a woman would not otherwise have had to connect with the perfect gentleman, didn't Penelope owe it to all women to do everything in her power to give them that chance?

"Balderdash," Saint Nick said flatly. "The whole point of earning something is to *earn* it. Not circumvent it with snake oil perfume or made-up science."

Her mouth fell open. "You don't believe in science?"

"How can anyone take it seriously?" he asked. "For centuries, alchemists have claimed they could turn lead into gold, purify the soul with mercury, cure consumption with an elixir. None of it has worked. These fools bumbling about as faux rakes are full of nothing more than false pretenses, just like the bottle those dreams were sold in."

The alarm went off, sending a rapid clockwork belt of three hundred nails pounding against a series of interlinked brass sheets connected to the closed door of her laboratory.

Penelope was glad for the distraction. She slid from her stool as if the unholy din wasn't vibrating through her bones, lifted the switch to stop the alarm, and strode to her oven.

Saint Nick might have meant his words to shock her. Or perhaps he thought *he* was the logical one, and she the poor befuddled female incapable of viewing the larger picture. Either way, she did not want him to see the excitement brimming in her blood. He had made a far more convincing argument than he even suspected.

Just not for the case he had in mind.

She slipped her wool-lined leather mitts over her hands and opened the oven door. Out of habit, she placed the tray of biscuits atop a cotton square designed for that purpose, and closed the oven door. But her mind was back in her laboratory.

Duchess had to be perfect. That was the only choice. It couldn't be as good as *Duke*. It had to surpass it.

But first, she had to prove the science. To show incontrovertible evidence that this new chemical combination worked exactly as advertised. All night, she had despaired of finding an unambiguous method of determining the latest compound's potency.

That was, until a non-believer walked through her door.

"Have a biscuit," she ordered.

He lifted his hand eagerly but then narrowed his eyes in suspicion. "I thought you said I had to leave when the alarm sounded."

"I only promised to listen to you until then." She tossed her leather mitts atop the counter and began to tidy the kitchen. "Are you peckish or not?"

The allure of fresh biscuits seemed to win out over his much-deserved suspicion. "May I have a plate?"

"Find one."

While her uninvited guest was thus occupied, Penelope slipped across the hallway into her laboratory to dab a drop of the working version of *Duchess* behind her ears and on her wrists.

Saint Nick was the perfect test subject. He didn't believe in perfume or science, but rather his own mind. Indeed, the deck was stacked delightfully against her.

He knew she was a perfumer. Believed she was the sort of alchemist who thought the right science could turn anything into something else. He would not trust her or her motives for a single second.

She was likewise a perfect control subject. Not only a spinster, not only a virgin, but one who had never been so much as flirted with before. If *Duchess* worked on Penelope, if it could win even the smallest token of affection from a rake who was already set against her, it would be an unarguable success.

'Twas the perfect experiment.

In order to prove her theory, Saint Nick needed to become overset with enough emotion to try to kiss her. Not that she would allow such a liberty.

For the kiss to be valid, it would need to be attempted for no reason other than him being unable to hold his passions at bay.

A peck of the cheek would not count. A brush of the lips against the back of her hand in greeting would not count. A manipulative wooing in an attempt to talk her into selling *Duke* would not count.

Only the sort of kiss that came from within would qualify. An unplanned kiss. The sort one fought against and only gave into when no choice remained but to indulge an overwhelming desire.

Not that Penelope had ever experienced any such event. She'd remained so far up on the shelf for so long that even wallflowers pitied her. She was old. Finished. She smirked. If the thought of kissing her were to cross any man's mind, it would be a miracle at thirty-four years.

Penelope didn't believe in miracles. She believed in science. Chemistry. Opportunity. It was time to start. She took a deep breath.

Well-meaning friends were always trying to get her to look different in order to be attractive, to *be* different in order to deserve love. Sweeter, flirtier, prettier. Become something men desired.

For this experiment to work, she was going to have to do the opposite. She narrowed her eyes. *Duchess* needed to let a woman bewitch a man without even trying.

First step: limit external influences.

There was no looking-glass in her laboratory, so she would have to do this part by feel. She tugged her already careless chignon a little more lopsided and tightened her battered smock about her neck. Next time, she would take care to make herself appear even more unappealing than usual. For now, she had to hurry. Saint Nick was bound to wonder where she was off to.

When she dashed back into the kitchen, she pulled up short. He was systematically demolishing biscuit after biscuit, consuming each with such care and sensual delight she quite doubted he had noticed her absence at all.

Her lips quirked at the sight. Although she hadn't baked the biscuits with Saint Nick in mind, she rather wished she had. Who knew watching a man consume something she created would be so satisfying?

"How are the biscuits?" she asked.

He jumped guiltily as if he'd forgotten Penelope altogether. She was not surprised. She hadn't been wearing *Duchess*. Now that she was, he would not forget her a second time.

"Does your offer still stand?" she asked.

He snuck the last crumb before setting his plate aside. "You'll sell me the rights to *Duke*?"

Under no circumstances. But Duchess needed time to work. Penelope was still refining the final characteristics. She didn't expect men to swoon at first sniff. Repeated exposure was the key. This could take days. She had to ensure he spent a measurable amount of time in scent range.

She leaned against the door jamb. "I promise to think it over. Come back tomorrow."

He abandoned the remaining biscuits with obvious remorse and reluctantly turned toward the doorway.

She was still standing there.

He could have squeezed past her.

She could have moved aside to give way.

Instead, they found themselves toe-to-toe, door jambs at their backs, with only a whisper of space between. Just enough room for *Duchess* to work.

"Thank you for the biscuits." He gave her a boyish smile.

She tried not to smile back. "Thank you for the flower."

"My pleasure." His eyes twinkled. "That is, until you left it lying on the ground like rubbish."

"It was rubbish," Penelope assured him. "Try harder next time."

His brow furrowed. "Try harder to what?"

"Whatever you're trying to do. Surprise me." There. *Duchess* should have reached his nostrils by now. Penelope moved out of arm's reach and motioned toward the door. "I'm sure the rose is still out there. There's time to give it to someone who would appreciate it."

"No," he said quietly, his blue eyes intense on hers. "You're right. The rose was meaningless. I'll do better."

But he made no move to exit.

Penelope's heart beat alarmingly fast. Something was happening. She tried to think rationally. A racing pulse was a good thing. Every beat of her heart was sending tiny pulses of *Duchess* from her pulse points to his nostrils. The scent was subtle. He would not know what was so intoxicating about her. It would just work.

She hoped.

Unfortunately, his scent was having an equally disruptive effect on her senses. This feeling of vertigo was not due to *Duke* or any other *eau de toilette*. She doubted he used one. He didn't have to. His scent was deeper than that, more real, more complex. A trace of his soap, the scent of his skin, an essence of arrogance and romance and danger. She swallowed hard.

Of course Saint Nick would not require cologne water. He was quite capable of being intoxicating all on his own.

At last, he dipped an extravagant bow followed by a cheeky grin. "Until tomorrow, Miss Mitchell."

"Until tomorrow," she murmured, unable to curtsy back.

He didn't so much as glance at the fallen rose as he strode back into the snow-covered streets and disappeared from view.

Penelope stood at the crack in her curtains for much longer. Her uneven breath steamed the window-glass until the wind stole away every last scarlet petal.

CHAPTER 5

*N*icholas prowled through Marlowe Castle's public dining area in search of his brother. Not Miss Mitchell, he reminded himself for the third time. His brother.

The castle perched on the zenith of the mountain served as more than an iconic landmark for the village of Christmas. It was the largest employer for the townsfolk, and *the* fashionable place to see and be seen.

Even before the town's late founder had bequeathed the castle to the villagers in a philanthropic trust, its grand dining hall had been available to all residents, free of charge.

Most took every meal in the castle in order to fraternize with their fellow neighbors. Meeting over a dinner table after a day's work or before an evening out was a fundamental component of local tradition. The residents thought of themselves not as a town, but as a family.

Nicholas's brother was exactly the sort of gentleman who would find romance in such quaint notions. Nicholas had little doubt that Chris was already imagining himself starting a family in a cozy, snow-frosted cottage with a crackling fireplace and a panoramic vista of evergreen-studded hills.

Nicholas was only staying until his planned fortnight was over. He'd set aside limited time for a holiday. Half was now gone. His fingers itched to get back to work. The last thing he should be doing was stalking through some castle dining hall in search of Penelope Mitchell.

Er, in search of his brother. Nicholas was *definitely* searching for Christopher. The rascal had to be here somewhere.

There he was!

Nicholas made his way to his brother's table and sat down beside him.

Chris stared at him as if he'd sprouted antlers and a bright red nose.

"What is it?" Nicholas growled in irritation.

His brother smirked. "If only I could say I've never seen so many women sigh in unison as you walk by. I just witnessed a room full of ladies flutter every possible fluttery thing. Eyelashes, fans, handkerchiefs, fichus… A peacock would be impressed with their ingenuity—and your stoicism," he added, impressed. "It truly looked as if you didn't notice any of it happening."

Nicholas cleared his throat. He *hadn't* noticed any of it happening. He'd been looking right through all the other castle guests in search of the only one that mattered.

His brother, of course. He had one hundred percent been looking for his brother.

"Perhaps I'm not interested," he said.

Chris nearly spit ale out his nose. "When are you ever uninterested in women? The very night we arrived here, you—"

Nicholas waved this away. "Ancient history."

"It was last week," Chris pointed out. "It's not like one becomes a different person overnight."

He had made no such transformation, Nicholas promised himself.

The only reason he had been plagued by troubled dreams last night was because his visit with Miss Mitchell had been unsettling. She had gotten under his skin.

Not that he was interested in her. His strict code of conduct did not allow emotional indulgences.

That she was the first woman he'd ever purposefully planned to see two days in a row did not signify. They weren't in the midst of an *affaire de cœur*. There was nothing between them at all, save for a potential business arrangement.

One with which Nicholas intended to shut down this *Duke* nonsense once and for all.

"What were you thinking about just now?" Chris asked curiously. "You had the strangest expression. As if you were trying to solve a puzzle but could not."

"No one. Nothing." Nicholas leaned back. "Have you found a bride yet?"

"I'll make my inquiries when they regain consciousness from swooning. Witnessing so much rakish presence in one room must be exhausting."

Nicholas frowned. His brother's mouth might have curved in jest, but there was no humor in his eyes.

"I'm sorry," Nicholas said contritely. "I didn't mean to distract the ladies."

"You never mean to. It's what you do." Chris shrugged. "It's fine. I'm used to it."

Nicholas glanced about the wide chamber.

Dozens of startled gazes immediately swung away, followed by a rustle of whispers.

"Five quid says they're working up the nerve to talk with me." Chris took a sip of his ale. "In order to beg an introduction to you."

A rock formed in Nicholas's stomach. "The sort of woman who would be interested in me is not the right bride for you."

"Even the sort that wasn't previously the sort, turns *into* the sort after she sees you," Chris said and finished his ale.

Nicholas slid the empty mug away from his brother. "How many of these have you had?"

"One," Chris answered. "I'm not sotted. I'm bored of living in your shadow. I am ready to take a wife. But you are the worst person to have along when a man is out bride-hunting. I give up."

"You can't give up," Nicholas said in horror. "You've always wanted to get married."

Chris toyed with his empty glass. "It's not as easy for me as it is for you. I can't walk up to a stranger and start talking."

Balderdash. Nicholas tried to understand. "Because you need a formal introduction first?"

"Because I don't know what to say."

"That's a lie. You've made more friends in the week we've been here than I've made in the past year."

"I'm not looking for friends," Chris muttered. "I knew you wouldn't understand. How has your morning gone? Have you been forced to commission a new bedpost to mark your conquests on?"

Nicholas tilted his head uncertainly at his brother. "You never seemed critical of my choices before."

"I've been critical of your choices since I could talk." Chris arched a brow. "I'm always telling you to stop wasting your time with the wrong women so you can find the right one."

"You never seemed *resentful* of my choices before," Nicholas clarified.

Chris shrugged. "You never paused your conquests long enough to notice. I haven't figured out why you're still sitting with me right now instead of sweeping one of these fine maidens off for the best hour or two of her life."

Did he truly seem that cavalier? Nicholas

swallowed a lump in his throat. The answer was clear.

Even at Oxford, the only times he and his brother saw each other were in social situations. Whenever Chris wasn't in class—or being dragged by Nicholas to some soirée or another —Chris was more likely to be found on a roof staring up through his telescope. Or staying up all night with the rest of the Junior Astronomers Club in hopes of glimpsing a shooting star or a new comet.

Or whatever aspiring astronomers did. Nicholas had no idea if comets and falling stars were the same thing.

He had his own interests. Interests he'd been too embarrassed to share with others. His brother knew, of course. Family was different. But even still, Nicholas had been happy to let everyone else believe he spent every possible moment dedicated to the fine art of wenching.

What had started as a convenient lie quickly took over his life.

Back at Eton, Nicholas had become the rake he'd pretended to be. And then he began to enjoy it. To revel in it. He liked the rules, the lines. "One night" was easy to understand. Fun. Predictable. Safe.

Becoming a rake had rescued him when he was adrift without direction. It had given him someone to be. Rules to live by. One night was not enough time to get to know another person. Not enough time to *like* them. To be vulnerable.

To have it all fall apart. Being a rake gave him control of his world.

He had never intended to ruin his brother's life in the process.

"Should I leave?" he asked quietly.

Chris shook his head. "You're paying for accommodations, too. Try the fish. I think you'll like the white sauce."

"I mean this village." Nicholas met his brother's eyes. "Should I leave?"

Chris let out a breath. "This is your holiday, too. Enjoy it."

"I'll be gone in a week," Nicholas promised. "Faster if I wrap up this business I'm trying to handle. In a few days, you'll be able to bride-hunt without my presence mucking up the works."

"You have actual business here?" His brother's eyes widened in shock. "Are you going to sell some of your—"

"No one knows about that," Nicholas said firmly. "Let's keep it that way."

"But you're good," Chris said. "One shouldn't keep one's talents a secret."

Nicholas's mouth curved dryly. "Some would say I don't."

"Not those talents." Chris rolled his eyes. "You should definitely keep those more secret. Give the rest of us a chance."

At that, Nicholas could not help but think of Miss Mitchell's words the previous afternoon. He straightened in alarm. "Please tell me you're not going to start bathing in *Duke* perfume."

"I said I agreed with you on the subject." Chris lifted a shoulder. "If I cannot woo a woman with honest romance, I shan't take her as my wife."

Nicholas blinked. "What the devil is 'honest romance?'"

"Romance that means something." His brother's eyes took on a far-off sheen. "Not a dozen roses, but her favorite flower. Not poetry from the masters, but some truly awful rhyming couplets that come from one's heart. Not an afternoon promenade to march her before all of London, but a hundred quiet moments that mean everything. Moments only the two of you would understand."

It was Nicholas's turn to stare at his brother as though he had sprouted antlers.

Good God. *Nicholas* wouldn't be engaging in any such behavior. Not only was romance for people who intended to see the same person again and again, it was an exercise in futility.

When Mother and Father's love match had turned sour, he and his brother had watched the drama unfold before their eyes. The snide comments. Long silences. Father's mistresses. The night Mother never came back.

Chris had sworn to do better.

Nicholas had vowed never to love at all. By far, the safer choice.

"You don't look convinced," Chris said.

Nicholas was very convinced. They just held opposing beliefs.

"Love isn't for me," he said. Even if he were to find it, it wouldn't last. He didn't need the heartbreak. But he wished his brother well. "Keep looking. You'll find her eventually."

And he would. If anyone deserved to find the love of a lifetime, it was his brother. Chris would do it right. He'd be better than their father. He'd start a romance that never ended.

"I wish you would change your mind," Chris said softly. "You can't live life in single-night segments forever."

Nicholas gave him a crooked grin. "Why not? If I sum all the 'one nights' together, it adds up to the same thing."

Sort of.

"At least do something you like," Chris suggested. "There's that smithy on the edge of town. Didn't you say they would rent it?"

Nicholas's fingers itched again. The le Duc smithy wouldn't be the same as home, but maybe it would be close. "That's a good idea. I'll try."

Chris gave an exaggerated shudder. "How can you stand crouching in front of a fireplace for hours at a time?"

Nicholas shrugged. "I like chimneys."

"You're mad," Chris said. "Raking has to be more fun."

With a hint of a smile, Nicholas rose from

the table and made his way out of the dining hall. A sliver of the afternoon was still free.

He had promised to meet Miss Mitchell again, but they hadn't formalized a certain hour. This errand would clear his head, give him time to think. Prepare him better than yesterday when she caught him so off-guard. He strode faster.

The smithy was a large wood-and-brick structure on the edge of the le Duc family property.

Nicholas knew little about the three siblings, save that they were French refugees fleeing Napoleon's regime, had become talented black-smiths, and were willing to rent Nicholas the entire workshop for an hour at a time, no questions asked.

Perhaps they needed the money. Or perhaps they *didn't* need the money, and preferred to spend the afternoon competing in one of their famed carriage races.

Nicholas was simply grateful for the borrowed space.

He stepped into the workshop and breathed in a warm, comforting mixture of iron, dust, and grease. His shoulders relaxed. The familiar scent alone was better than any massage.

Today he was not here to work, but to explore. Inspect the arrangement, test the equipment, gauge the privacy. He walked about the interior, taking his time.

He could only imagine the fun the caricaturists would have if it ever came out that Nicholas Pringle, avowed rake and man-about-town, spent every moment outside the London Season holed up in a private workshop not unlike this one, creating art from boiling glass and red-hot metal.

It would be the death of his reputation. Death of the life he had built for himself. Glass-blowing and mold-casting were not the activities of a Casanova, but the pastime of a recluse just as happy with his hands covered in calluses as in dancing gloves.

By Jove, was this a wonderful workshop. Nicholas had missed smelling of bronze and fire. Hated being away from his forge, his kiln. He spent long minutes inspecting each shelf, and the treasures it contained. This was exactly what he needed.

No amount of riding in Hyde Park or boxing at Gentleman Jackson's or fencing with members of his club came close to the sensation of tumbling into bed at night after spending the entire day hard at work on his glass.

Nicholas did nothing with his creations, of course. Locked them in a wardrobe to gather dust. What else was he to do? He had no pretensions of becoming an *artiste*. That wasn't what the world wanted from him.

But it didn't mean he had to give it up completely. Not even here in Christmas. His pulse sang with joy as he inspected the workshop. It was perfect. Next time he would not rent it for an hour, but an afternoon. Or perhaps all night long. Once he started on a project, he was likely to forget all about time and—

Miss Mitchell! She was expecting him. He pulled out his pocket watch and grimaced. The hour had grown late so quickly. With a last glance toward the kiln, he forced himself to quit the smithy. He would come back soon. In the meantime, he didn't want to miss his opportunity to convince Miss Mitchell to sell *Duke*.

As he hurried back toward the street, a tiny stone caught his eye. Intrigued, he bent to pick it up. As big as a strawberry and as smooth as a grape, its oblong surface glittered in the late afternoon sun as if dusted with fool's gold. Nicholas grinned.

The color reminded him of Miss Mitchell's eyes. Complex. Full of mystery. More beautiful than they were given credit for. He rubbed the pad of his thumb across the pretty stone, then shoved it into his pocket, irritated with his flight of fancy.

Those were precisely the sort of foolish thoughts Father had castigated him for as a child. Rocks weren't *pretty*. A man's sons needn't always behave like gentlemen, but they ought to be *manly*, for God's sake. Did Nicholas want to be the laughingstock of Eton?

No, Nicholas had not wished to be the laughingstock of anywhere. Out of necessity, he'd learned to keep his inside separate from his outside. Make friends, seduce women, become the sort of man his father could be proud of. Publicly, at least.

Only his brother knew that Nicholas still dabbled with molten glass. But even Chris had not seen many of the painstaking creations. It was better that way. Easier. Nicholas couldn't disappoint people if they didn't know who he truly was.

He adjusted the rakish angle of his hat and strode up Miss Mitchell's front walk. As before, she was the one who answered his knock.

Today, she looked as though she had lost a battle with a fire-breathing dragon.

Her leather boots were badly scuffed. Her linen frock was worn at the elbows and missing half of its trim. Her thick gray smock was stained with every color imaginable, and featured three suspiciously large holes that appeared to have been singed with some sort of corrosive liquid. Her oversized gloves were burnt in odd places, as if she'd put out a runaway fire by smacking at it with her hands.

Her hair was mostly clumped together in some sort of knot that hung precariously to one side, a forgotten pencil poking haphazardly from tangled curls. One freckled cheekbone was streaked with the remnants of white powder, and a tiny spot of soot marred the tip of her nose. He grinned.

She looked positively magnificent.

Like a Greek painting come to life. A capricious goddess who cared not one whit what mere mortals thought of her. She didn't hide. Wasn't ashamed to be herself at all. The concept was as baffling as it was intoxicating.

"You smell like biscuits," he blurted.

"They're cold." She narrowed her eyes at him reprovingly. "You're late."

He pulled up short. "Did we agree upon a time?"

She craned her neck to peer behind him. "No flowers today?"

"You don't like flowers," he reminded her.

"Everyone likes flowers," she said with a laugh.

He shook his head. "You didn't like the one *I* brought."

"You didn't mean it. I believe you promised you'd do better." She leaned against the doorframe and crossed her arms. "Did you?"

Nicholas shifted his weight. He *had* said that, and then promptly forgot. Blast. Nothing he'd ever said had mattered the second day before. "Er..."

"As I thought." She moved out of the way. "Come on in, Mr. Disappointment."

"Wait. I brought you this." The stone was in his hand before he could stop himself.

She stared at it without changing expression. "It's a rock."

He nodded. "Yes."

Her forehead creased. "You brought me a rock instead of flowers."

"Yes," he said again, wishing very much that he had not. "I'll get rid of it."

He began to curl his fingers about the stone in order to toss it over his shoulder in embarrassment.

She clasped her gloved hands about his fist before he could do so. "Don't. I like it."

He didn't move.

She didn't lift her hands from his.

His heart gave a strange lurch.

"You like rocks better than flowers?" he asked uncertainly.

"I like *this* rock." She pried it from his hand and dropped it into the bib pocket of her smock. "You meant it. Well done." She motioned toward the drawing room fireplace. "Your biscuits are on the mantel."

"Er... Thank you." He stepped inside and took off his hat. "Have you had enough time to consider my proposal?"

Too late.

She was gone.

Perhaps he had interrupted her in the midst of some experiment. No doubt she had disappeared to her dressing room in order to put herself to rights.

'Twas of no import. He had a moment to spare. After all, there were biscuits. He hurried over to the mantel where a stack of half a dozen rose from a single saucer.

"Don't mind if I do," he murmured, and lifted

the first biscuit to his mouth. Mmm. Raisin and oat. He let his eyes close in happiness.

"Do they meet your approval?"

He spun around, neck growing hot. "That was fast. I expected you to—"

Change seemed an inopportune word if he still hoped to sweet-talk her out of *Duke*'s custody. It seemed Miss Mitchell had not gone to freshen up. She had gone to fetch more biscuits.

Nicholas much preferred this turn of events.

"These have cranberries," she said. "You may only have one. I'm working on a new recipe for the reception hall."

He lifted it from the tray with reverence. Some opined that the greatest magic of the local area was year-round Christmastide nestled high in a winter wonderland.

For Nicholas, the magic had begun when he and his brother walked into the castle's receiving area and were immediately greeted by an enormous buffet featuring spiced wine and tall platters of fresh biscuits.

With a crooked grin, he lifted his now-empty saucer. "These are delectable. I am happy to test as many recipes as you please."

She plucked the dish from his hand. "I'm done baking. I am far too busy to waste time on more than one new recipe a week."

A new recipe every week? Nicholas's breath caught. He was beginning to regret limiting his holiday to a single fortnight.

"Much too busy doing what?" he asked. With her, it could be anything.

"Experiments." She made a gesture toward the corridor. "In my laboratory."

At least he had guessed something right. He had begun to think he would never know what to expect with her.

Debutantes fit a certain pattern, courtesans another, the widows and fallen women who sought to spend their nights in the arms of a lover were yet another.

Miss Mitchell was different. If spinsters and bluestockings were supposed to be dull, she had broken that mold. She knew her own mind. She didn't need Nicholas or anyone. He doubted she even allowed Mother Nature to get in her way.

"Have you considered my proposal?" he asked anyway.

"Yes." She gave a brisk nod. "The answer is no."

"Any price," he reminded her with his most gallant smile. "Just name it."

She gave him a consoling look. "I don't need your money. I have my own."

"I could give you more." He no longer knew why he was so desperate for her to say yes. Was it to finally put paid to the ridiculous rakelings crawling out of the woodwork? Or was it so he would have an excuse to come back and see her? "What would it take for you to stop producing *Duke?*"

Her brow furrowed in thought as she considered the question carefully. "The apocalypse?"

A soft snort of laughter escaped before he could stifle it. He supposed he'd expected as much, but it had been worth the shot. "So definitely no?"

"Definitely no," she said firmly and motioned her free hand toward the door.

The startled laugh that escaped his throat this time held no humor at all.

He had never been dismissed from a woman's home before. The sensation was unnerving. He might not be a member of Parliament or a great inventor, but all the other ladies of his acquaintance had managed to put him to good use.

Nicholas frowned to realize that was not precisely what he wanted from Miss Mitchell. What on earth was happening? His throat tightened as he turned toward the door.

Perhaps her disinterest in making a good impression was what made Nicholas want to make a good impression on *her*. Or perhaps it was her surprising acceptance of a simple stone as a gift that made him wish he had more to offer.

What would it be like to have someone want to spend time with *him*, not just his body? To be able to be the person he truly was, not the person everyone expected to see?

A nightmare, he reminded himself firmly. He had built his walls for a reason. They kept him safe. Miss Mitchell was dangerous.

She followed him to the door and leaned one slim shoulder against the frame as he made his way out into the fading light. "If I ever catch you hanging about my doorstep again..."

He paused and glanced over his shoulder, eyebrows raised.

She grinned at him. "There may be biscuits."

The door shut tight before he could respond. Not that he was capable. He was smiling too widely to think of anything brilliant to say. To his surprise, the villagers had been right.

Coming here really did feel like Christmas.

CHAPTER 6

*P*enelope leaned against the wainscoting beside her friend Miss Virginia Underwood. From an unobtrusive corner, they watched guests wander in and out of the castle. Penelope was keeping tally-marks of which sorts of guests chose which biscuits.

Virginia was trying to impart an important lesson upon her. Or perhaps recounting a half-remembered dream. With Virginia, sometimes it was hard to tell.

"And although the noble turtledove can survive on its own," she was saying, "it is with both its mate and the rest of its flock that it thrives."

Penelope glanced at her sharply. "Are we talking about birds or about me? I have my flock. I don't need a mate."

Virginia sent her a sorrowful look. "You're keeping tally-marks of biscuit selection."

"That doesn't negate the point," Penelope muttered. "Observation is a key component of my methodology. The castle staff can report how many biscuits were consumed overall, but they won't know which people ate which ones, or how many, or under what circumstances no biscuits were chosen at all."

"Why do you need to know?" Virginia asked. "You provide the recipe and the kitchen bakes the biscuits. Whichever type is more popular, they will bake more of. Why must it be more complicated than that?"

"Aren't you curious?" Penelope asked. "If I told you men old enough to grow beards were less likely to choose lemon, and that blond children in pairs tended to choose cinnamon over nutmeg, wouldn't you want to know why?"

Virginia's eyes widened. "Is that true?"

"I don't know." Penelope lifted up her notebook. "I must observe and tally in order to find out."

Virginia harrumphed. "Is this your attempt to replace one obsession with another?"

"What?" Penelope stammered.

Virginia raised her brows. "Do you care a single fig about biscuit consumption, or are you hoping to spy a specific biscuit consumer?"

"What?" Penelope said again.

Virginia had an atrocious habit of being perceptive.

Penelope busied herself with her notebook.

"Spread your wings," Virginia suggested. "Show your true colors. The turtledove—"

"He is not some bird-mate," Penelope snapped. "He's a very bad idea."

"*Ohh*," Virginia said knowingly, as if this slip had given away everything. It probably had. "I understand. You're afraid he'll return to his own nest."

"I *know* he'll fly south. He's a migratory bird." Penelope slammed down her pencil and glared at her friend. "See what you did? Now I'm talking like you."

Virginia crossed her arms. "What do the others say?"

"I have not asked anyone's opinion," Penelope enunciated clearly.

Virginia continued undaunted. "What do others say to women who do seek advice?"

"You've heard it all before. To attract a man, one must style one's hair like this, commission a gown like that, flutter one's eyes, swing one's hips, speak in a breathy little baby voice, but only when spoken to." Penelope snorted. "It's hogwash."

"Utter hogwash," Virginia agreed. "You made the right choice by looking as drab as possible."

Penelope blinked. "I look what?"

"After all," Virginia continued, "It is the male who must attract his mate. The robin's red breast, the peacock's plumage, the lion's mane. Beauty is *their* role. Your job is not to be desirable, but to be desired."

"Well, it's not working," Penelope muttered.

She'd spent all day in her laboratory with the

door cracked open in order to be able to hear any fortuitous raps upon the knocker outside.

None had come.

Perhaps she hadn't worn quite enough *Duchess* yesterday afternoon. Perhaps Saint Nick was immune to her scent, faux or otherwise. Perhaps there were too many factors outside her control. Perhaps the experiment was over before it truly began.

"What's wrong?" Virginia asked, her brow furrowed in concern.

"I'm working on a new perfume," Penelope admitted. "It's not going well."

Virginia's eyes sparkled in understanding. "You don't want a mate. You'd like *to* mate."

"*Shh.*" Penelope darted her gaze about the entrance hall to ensure no one had overheard. "Fine. I wouldn't sob if he kissed me. But it's not going to happen. Worse, he wants me to stop what I'm doing."

Virginia nodded in commiseration. "He wants you to stop looking drab?"

"He wants me to stop using science." Penelope's teeth clenched. "He wants me to throw away my greatest success. He thinks it's a failure. A monster that should never have existed."

"He is probably smitten," Virginia said. "Men say the stupidest things when they're in love."

"He's not in love," Penelope burst out. "I doubt he believes in it any more than I do."

Virginia lifted her brows. "When has belief in love ever stopped it from happening?"

Penelope shook her head. "He lives for pleasure. I live for science. We're incompatible."

"Change your experiment," Virginia said. "Tally your observations of people in love until you prove to yourself it exists."

"I can't prove it's *forever*," Penelope said after a moment. "One can observe instances where love does not last, but not predict with any certainty when it will."

Virginia tilted her head. "Then what can you prove?"

"Desire," Penelope said simply. "All animals share an impulse to mate with one another. Yet they do not mate with all individuals of their kind. They choose. It is the selection process that interests me. If it can be influenced by chemistry, I will find a way to do so."

"Oh." Virginia cocked a brow. "You want to be the chosen biscuit. That's why you're tallying."

Penelope let out a frustrated sigh. "I do not want to be a…"

Did she? As soon as she'd heard the knock upon her door yesterday afternoon, she had dabbed on extra drops of *Duchess* for the experiment. Not for emotional reasons.

"I see." Virginia gave a smile of commiseration. "You don't want to just be part of the selection. You want to be the burnt biscuit that gets chosen first anyway."

Penelope glared at her friend.

Virginia had the strangest way of phrasing

almost everything, but she was very rarely wrong.

Penelope *was* burnt. Drab. Left out cold. Crumbling at the edges. But she needed to be, for the perfume trial. Her clients would want to be chosen first. They would expect *Duchess* to help them achieve it. If such a feat could happen for Penelope, it could be recreated for anyone. Chemistry in a bottle.

Virginia lifted Penelope's wrist and sniffed. "Is that why you are drabber than usual?"

Penelope yanked her wrist out of Virginia's grasp. "Is 'drabber' a word?"

"There isn't a word for..." Virginia waved a hand in the direction of Penelope's carefully chosen attire. "*This.*"

"Yes, if you must know. To prove the effect is due to the perfume, I must be unattractive in every other way. I can wear the oldest, most comfortable clothes in my wardrobe—"

"This particular frock should be incinerated."

"—I can amuse myself spending an hour to make my hair as frizzy and lopsided as possible—"

"It doesn't look like you remembered it was on your head at all."

"—and I needn't bother attempting to be graceful or coquettish or sultry. It's quite free-ing. Why are you being so negative about it?"

"You're assuming the only way to attract a man is something you do with your body." Virginia cocked her head. "What if he likes your brain?"

"No man has ever liked a woman's brain. They're not even convinced we possess them," Penelope said dryly.

Virginia appeared to think this over. "He said *Duke* doesn't work?"

"He said it does work," Penelope clarified. "That's what he hates about it."

"Then he knows you have a brain." Virginia leaned back against the wainscoting and closed her eyes. "You should get a pet."

Penelope gazed up at the heavens for strength. "What would be the point of a pet?"

Virginia sighed happily. "Something to love."

"I told you," Penelope said. "I don't believe in love."

"Something to love *you*." Virginia opened her eyes and clapped her hands with excitement. "I have an extra bird."

"I do not want a bird," Penelope said quickly. "Do not give me a bird."

Virginia narrowed her eyes. "Are you afraid the bird won't like you?"

"I don't care if birds like me."

"Are you afraid the bird won't *choose* you?" Virginia insisted.

"I do not want any bird to choose me."

"Everyone cares when they're not chosen."

"I don't," Penelope said firmly. "If interest in another person is driven by chemistry rather than personal connection, the lack of it in one's life cannot reflect negatively on oneself."

"Ohh." Virginia nodded sagely. "You don't want to prove there's a lack in yourself."

"Are you trying to make me feel worse or better?" Penelope burst out. "You're doing a terrible job. If I tallied every single time you—"

"Put your plumage away," Virginia hissed. "Here comes your peacock."

Penelope jerked her spine up straight before she remembered she was trying to be slumpy and frumpy on purpose.

Too late. Saint Nick had seen her.

He and his brother were heading directly their way.

"Miss Mitchell." He sketched an elegant bow. "Allow me to present my brother, Mr. Christopher Pringle."

His brother bowed. "Do call me Christopher. Two Mr. Pringles are too many."

Saint Nick's smile widened. "I, of course, am Nicholas. Who is this lovely lady at your side?"

Penelope swallowed. Was she supposed to curtsy? She definitely wasn't going to curtsy. She was being dowdy and unattractive. "Virginia, meet... Nick and Christopher. Gentlemen, this is Miss Virginia Underwood."

Virginia clasped her hands to her chest. "I am glad the winds blew you this way."

Christopher frowned, then laughed in appreciation. "You mean to the refreshment table? All winds blow Nicholas toward biscuits. But when he saw you and Miss Mitchell, we had to ensure you ladies were enjoying your evening."

Virginia elbowed Penelope in the ribs. "Happy? He chose the burnt biscuit."

Penelope nudged her boot and hissed back, "Not now, Virginia."

Saint Nick smiled. "Chris informs me that only a fool would miss seeing the stars tonight, because there's a…" He pretended to think, and then shrugged. "I can never recall words longer than two syllables. My brother swears the sky will be lovely. Care to step outside with us and put his theory to the test?"

"Penelope loves theories," Virginia said. "Right now, she's working on—"

"By all means," Penelope said quickly. "I adore nature and multi-syllable words. Your brother sounds fascinating."

"You're right." Christopher grinned at Nicholas. "She *is* a spitfire."

"He talked about the biscuit," Virginia whispered in excitement.

"Stop it," Penelope whispered back.

"Satan," Nicholas corrected with a straight face. "If you wish to quote me correctly, I said she was Satan incarnate for having brought the latest plague upon England."

"Satan," Christopher mused. "No, it was a different synonym. 'Devilish tempting,' was it?"

"I will not help you find a wife if you keep meddling in my affairs," Nicholas scolded his brother. He turned to Penelope. "I did not call you tempting—"

"Or Satan," Christopher put in with a smile.

"—but I may have referred to your perfume as a plague on more than one occasion."

"On all possible occasions," Christopher added with a long-suffering grimace.

Virginia enveloped Penelope in a hug. "Your perfume is an even bigger success than I dreamed. Congratulations on your first plague."

"Her... first plague?" Christopher prompted in concern.

"Aren't there some stars we're supposed to be seeing?" Penelope asked. "A bit difficult to do whilst still inside the castle."

"Quite right, quite right." Christopher proffered his elbow to Virginia. "If the mortal enemies will follow behind?"

Nicholas offered Penelope his arm and a grin. "My apologies. Chris loves stars the way wiser men love biscuits."

"Your brother is delightful," she replied as she took his arm. There. That would prove she wasn't giving any special attention to Nicholas.

"He is wearing a new waistcoat," he whispered. "Compliment him on it."

Penelope narrowed her eyes in his brother's direction. "It looks like the one you wore two days ago."

"New to him," Nicholas corrected. "Compliment him anyway."

She made a mental note to do so. "Is he really looking for a wife?"

"He really is." Nicholas groaned, as if the pursuit was on par with running off to become a sword-swallower in a circus.

A sudden thought soured her stomach. "You're not trying to matchmake me off to him, are you?"

Nicholas stopped so suddenly, Penelope nearly crashed into him. His eyes were unreadable. "No. I am definitely not trying to do that."

Because he couldn't stand the thought of her with his brother? Or because he didn't think her worthy of marriage? She was gently born, and had inherited a comfortable annuity. Her life might not be as ostentatious as his usual crowd, but she was still respectable.

Penelope clenched her teeth. She shouldn't care. She didn't want to marry Christopher, Nicholas, or anyone. Their thoughts on her eligibility were completely irrelevant. All that mattered was the experiment.

Yet the uncertainty lingered.

When they stepped outside, the wind whipped away any other words she might say before she could have a chance to regret them. 'Twas better that way. The night was cold. The air was brisk, but not freezing. She stayed flush with Nicholas's warm side as she angled her head back to gaze up at the stars.

"Incredible," she breathed. Without a cloud in the sky, their view from the mountaintop was a perfect blanket of stars all around them. "Do you find it beautiful?"

Nicholas didn't say a word.

She tilted her head toward his and blinked to discover his hooded gaze on her, rather than the heavens. Her heart pounded.

They were standing too close. Their mouths were now inches apart. If he lowered his head or she rose on her toes, their lips could touch.

Her entire body tingled with proximity and awareness. She forgot about the stars, the castle, the cold. Her body had never felt warmer. Every molecule felt feverishly alive.

She needed to regain perspective posthaste.

Her rapid heartbeat was the cause of her elevated core temperature, she reminded herself. Her body's reaction to the signs of *Duchess*'s success. Not to Nicholas.

But it was no use. Of course it was him. Frozen, just like her. Not from cold, but from heat. The look in his eyes said he'd very much like to kiss her. That he was considering it even still. That he was as surprised as she was, but the shock had not extinguished the desire. She held her breath and waited.

Had his head lowered a tiny fraction? Were their mouths a little closer than they were before?

There was nothing Penelope wanted more than to rise up on her toes in order to give him easier access. To give him a sign. Give him—

"Do you see Cassiopeia?" Christopher called

out from somewhere up ahead. "She is still a goddess of beauty."

The moment shattered. Penelope and Nicholas jerked their faces away from each other and up toward the sky as if nothing had happened.

Something had definitely happened.

Penelope's heart would not stop racing. It was her first almost-kiss. *Duchess* was working! Her breath caught. If his brother hadn't been a few yards ahead, if they hadn't been standing within sight of the castle, Nicholas might have lowered his mouth to hers and kissed her.

That was the next step, then. An almost-kiss wasn't the same as a kiss. She would adjust the formula and try again. If Nicholas kissed her—for no reason at all, other than wanting to kiss her—*Duchess* would be a success. She was almost there.

Her entire body thrilled at being so close to winning. Or maybe it thrilled at still being flush against the warm side of the handsome rake who had almost kissed her.

Her fingers still trembled where they curved about his arm. Her chest tightened. Devil take it, she was having a physical reaction! *Duchess* was designed to work on men, not women, which meant her body was responding this way because of... Nicholas.

Drat. She gritted her teeth. His biology must be a match for hers. Or perhaps his unique chemistry made him a universal attractor to women. She sighed. No wonder he was such a successful rake.

No matter. She could not allow emotion to get in the way of science. She would have to stay strong. Stoic. Tonight's marginal success would be an incremental tally in her notebook, and nothing more.

CHAPTER 7

*N*icholas's fingers were still on the knocker when the door swung open.

Miss Mitchell smiled at him approvingly. "You're early."

He raised his brows. "Did we agree on a time?"

"I'll be in the kitchen." Her eyes twinkled at him before she disappeared from view.

He stepped inside the house and shut the door behind him. For the first time since arriving in Christmas, he had no need to stomp the snow from his feet before entering. Today was almost warm, and much of the snow had melted from the streets and walkways.

He hung his hat and coat on the rack near the door and crossed over to the mantel. No biscuits awaited, but from the rich, cinnamon-sugar smell of the cottage, they would be arriving at any moment.

Nicholas grinned. Miss Mitchell was right. He was early.

He reached into his pocket and pulled out a delicate glass disc in the shape of a flower petal. He had made it just that morning. He turned it over in his hand.

On its own, it didn't look like much. Certainly nothing like the flower he'd modeled it after. The smooth slip of glass could be a curl of anything. A scrap of nothing. Or a single glass petal. He placed it on the mantel where a saucer of biscuits had stood once before.

The glass disc was scarcely visible from a distance. A nearly invisible echo of the rose he'd brought and tossed aside because its intended recipient held no interest in meaningless gifts. Nicholas agreed. She deserved something genuine.

Glass was better than a rose. It didn't need water, wouldn't wilt, wasn't slowly dying after being cut off from its roots so that its beauty might be appreciated from the comfort of one's home.

This single petal would stay perfect forever. It would remain beautiful and whole long after Nicholas returned home and left Christmas behind.

He turned his back to the mantel and made his way into the kitchen.

The moment he took a seat on one of the wooden stools, Miss Mitchell pulled a tray of biscuits from the oven and placed it on a square towel atop the table.

"Let them set for twelve minutes," she said. "Then you can eat them."

"All of them?" He leaned toward them with interest.

Her lips twitched. "If you do, you'll be too full to try the new recipe."

"There's no such thing as 'too full' to eat biscuits," he protested.

"We'll see." She gave him a knowing look. "I'm making two dozen."

He placed his palm over his heart. "I solemnly pledge to do my very best to consume—"

"The other batch isn't for you," she said with a shake of her finger. "They're for your brother."

His mouth fell open. "*Christopher* gets the biscuits?"

"Christopher's potential love interests get the biscuits," she corrected. "He's to hand them out at will. It should work. The only thing miserable, corseted young ladies love more than biscuits is a man who lets her eat them."

He raised a brow. "Do you consider yourself a miserable, corseted young lady?"

"No on all four counts," she answered cheerfully. "I prefer biscuits to corsets, and I'm quite pleased to have made that decision. At four-and-thirty, I'm too old to be young. No need for pity. I consider myself a woman of science, not a spinster."

"You're four-and-thirty?" he repeated in surprise.

She curtsied. "Are you appalled?"

"I should hope not," he said. "Not when I'm six-and-thirty. We've got decades of 'young' ahead of us."

She leaned one hip against the table. "It's easier for men. You're not born with a 'wed-by' date. All your bits work indefinitely."

"Is 'bits' a scientific term?"

"It's the 'proper young lady' term. I am happy to use more precise vocabulary. Shouldn't we call things as they are properly named?"

"I'm not certain it is proper to refer to a man's—" he cleared his throat "—*bits,* regardless of terminology."

Her eyes shone with laughter. "Never say you are shocked and offended."

"Not in the least," he assured her. "I am always pleased when my bits are of interest. We can discuss their attributes in as much depth as you like."

"I'm fairly certain most of England has heard all they need to know about your bits," she said wryly and held out her palm. "Flour, please."

He started and reflexively touched the empty pocket where he'd kept the glass petal. "I didn't bring—"

"Right behind you. Two cups, if you please."

He glanced over his shoulder and then back to her. "You want me to measure the baking flour?"

"I intend for you to measure all the ingredients." She affected an imperious stance. "'He who ate them, baked them.'"

He stared at her. "I am... fairly certain that's not a phrase."

"I just coined it." She wiggled her fingers toward the counter. "Are you done measuring?"

He leapt up from his stool and rushed to the bag of flour. "What do I measure with?"

"Bring it here. I'll show you."

For the next half hour, they worked side-by-side.

Nicholas had no doubt the mixing of the batter took twice as long with him helping, but he had never had more fun. The flour dusting both their clothes, the smudge of butter on her cheek, every brush of her fingers against his as she showed him how to mix the dough. He grinned to himself.

Baking biscuits was his new favorite pastime.

When the first tray was finally ready for the oven, he was surprised to realize that he'd forgotten all about the original dozen cooling on the table. Those twelve minutes had long since elapsed. His eyes widened. He'd been too busy enjoying his time with Miss Mitchell to bother eating shortbread biscuits. What on earth was happening?

Miss Mitchell perched on a stool and popped one of the biscuits into her mouth. "First time in the kitchen?"

"I've been in scads of kitchens," he protested.

"First time making something edible?"

"The biscuits are still in the oven," he reminded her. "We'll have to see."

"It's a good skill for you to develop," she said. "If you offer nice enough biscuits, perhaps people will still visit you after your good looks are gone."

He choked on his biscuit. "After my what?"

"It's nature," she said. "*Human* nature. Your features will never lose their appealing symmetry. But at some point, the rest of you will fail to meet the prevailing beauty standards. Perhaps you will be too fat or too skinny. Too bald or too hairy." She cocked her head. "Men do tend to sprout hairs from all sorts of interesting places as they get older."

"Is this another reference to my bits?" he asked. "I promise they haven't been sprouting anything."

Besides, there was no need to learn how to bake. His staff most certainly included a cook. If he wished to entertain at home, there would be no shortage of biscuits.

"You need a hobby," she continued. "Once the whole rake boom dries up, you'll need something to do."

He *had* something to do. A secret life, forging molten glass into works of art that would never fade or age. That side of him would have to stay private. The *ton* would never comprehend how menial tasks could bring so much joy. They would laugh him right out of London.

Miss Mitchell understood. She had a maid on staff fully capable of baking, but preferred to get her hands dirty herself. She thought he could be more than just a rake.

Then again, she was also an eccentric lady chemist living in a remote village in the northernmost corner of all of England. In such unusual circumstances, an independently wealthy spinster could be as peculiar as she pleased.

Nicholas did not share that freedom. His hobby would have to remain a secret. If anything, he did his best to ensure that life as he knew it would never change at all.

"Your vision of me in the future is some fat, balding, white-bearded old man who sits around eating biscuits?" he enquired politely.

She lifted her brows. "What's *your* vision of yourself in the future?"

He stared back at her without responding. Truth be told, he'd been concentrating too hard on each day as it passed to bother worrying about what the future held.

Her prediction terrified him. His looks were all he had. What would he be when they were gone? It would happen. Someday he would be too old or too tired or too roly-poly from excess biscuit consumption to carry on as he was now. He'd end up spending every day in his workshop. Alone.

Was loneliness his inevitable fate? Being a rake didn't fulfill any deep passion. It passed the days. Or more precisely, the nights. It gave him a part to play in the society he lived in. When that role was gone, perhaps his part in society would disappear with it. Perhaps he would cease to matter, too.

He forced the thought away and returned his focus to Miss Mitchell. "Where do you see yourself in the future?"

Her eyes lit up at once. "In my laboratory, inventing something new. On stage, accepting an award for breakthroughs in science. In London, finally presenting my work to the Natural Philosophers Society."

"You don't do that now?" he asked in surprise. "I could picture you lecturing them every day of the week."

Her smile turned brittle. "Membership is closed to lady chemists."

"Imbeciles," he said immediately. "Your left toe is more brilliant than any of those short-sighted fools."

"You haven't met my left toe," she reminded him, lips quirking.

He wiggled his brows. "Would you like to show it to me?"

"I'd be happy to kick you with it," she replied sweetly.

"I'd let you," he said with a grin. "I like a woman who knows what she wants."

"As long as the thing she wants is you?" she asked dryly.

"Or biscuits," he said, but his throat was now tight.

For the second time in the same conversation, her unveiled allusion to his rakish reputation caused a twinge of guilt. He knew she was teasing. If ever there was a woman who would find no fault in obeying the body's urges, that woman was Miss Penelope Mitchell. And yet Nicholas could not help but wish she was wrong about him. That he could do better. That he could *be* better.

It was unfamiliar ground. None of his previous interactions with women had involved much talking, much less quiet introspection and meaningful revelations. He'd had encounters, not relationships.

She was forcing him to change all that.

Somehow, they had become friends. Or something far more complicated.

When Chris had asked if Nicholas had ever had a day so perfect he'd wished all others were like it, the answer had been no.

Yet he'd returned to this cottage several days in a row, with the express purpose of repeating the previous day's delightful banter and delicious biscuits. His brother was wrong. With her, each day wasn't the same. It was better than the last. He hadn't expected to pour out cups of sugar and flour, squish it all together with eggs and butter, his forehead bumping hers between giggles as they bent over the same bowl of batter.

In that moment, he'd wanted nothing more than to kiss her. He could think of nothing else.

Yet he also didn't want to ruin what they had. He wanted to be able to come back. He wanted whatever tomorrow might bring.

A horrific, mind-deadening racket filled the air. Miss Mitchell calmly rose to her feet. Nicholas narrowly avoided apoplexy. He would never get used to that alarm.

She switched off the noise and pulled the biscuits out of the oven.

"Let them cool," she warned him firmly. "Twelve minutes."

He widened his eyes innocently. "How ever could two young, stunningly attractive people with the perfect amount of hair, possibly pass twelve long minutes?"

"I've an idea." She walked out of the kitchen and crossed into an adjoining room. "Coming?"

Her idea was unlikely to be the same as his, but he was up for adventure.

He followed her into what was apparently her laboratory. It was filled with perfectly organized tools and flasks of every shape and size.

His spirits soared. He loved workshops. He wondered what she might think of his. This one was marvelous. He gazed about with pleasure. One section of the workbench held a project clearly in progress.

He edged closer with interest. "What's this?"

"*Duchess,*" she answered. "I'm on iteration twenty-seven point five."

He blinked. "*Duchess?*"

"A perfume for women," she explained as she

took a seat before a row of glass vials. "Men shouldn't have all the fun."

"You're making *Duke* for ladies," he repeated. Good God. It *was* the apocalypse.

She nodded. "*Duchess*. I've been working on the formula for months."

He swallowed his panic. "How does one work on a formula?"

"Field tests." She made an exaggerated pout and fluttered her eyelashes. "I tally how many gentlemen swoon at my feet."

An unreasonable surge of searing jealousy shot through him. No man could resist her. And now, with this…

He stared aghast at the slender vials. Perfume was perfume. It could not be targeted toward a single source. If the new concoction worked half as well as *Duke*, she would have to wield an umbrella about to shield herself from all the smitten swains.

The strange sensation in his stomach didn't go away. How many tally marks would that be? Nicholas might be heir presumptive to a dukedom he was unlikely to inherit, but he was far from the only gentleman in town.

The Duke of Azureford famously had a cottage right here in the village. Azureford! An actual handsome, single duke who did not require *eau de toilette* to attract young ladies. He was unequivocally the better catch.

"Are you going to sit?" she asked.

He sat.

There was no reason to be jealous, he told himself. Azureford had always been the better man. Almost everyone was. Nicholas wasn't the marrying type. He wasn't even going to stay in Christmas. His feelings were irrelevant. What Miss Mitchell did on her own time had absolutely nothing to do with him.

"I don't like it," he said.

"How do you know?" She lifted the stopper from a vial. "Would you like to smell it?"

He wanted to stop it. This was worse than *Duke*.

"Sell me exclusive production rights," he said quickly. "Name your price."

She lowered her nose to the vial. "Why do you think everything can be bought?"

Clearly it could not. He would have to find some other way to halt its production.

"If you're just going to glower at me over my shoulder, then you might as well go back into the kitchen." She stoppered the vial and placed it back with its siblings. "I knew having a guest in here would be a bad idea."

His heart skipped at her words. He stared at her speechlessly. She had brought the stool in for him. He was the first person she'd allowed in her private space. And he was about to lose that privilege due to a raging case of illogical jealousy.

"I'll stay," he said quickly. "I've finished glowering. Tell me what you do with these vials. Do you measure with them, like we did for the biscuits?"

"Not like the biscuits at all," she said with a chuckle. "The ones over here…"

So began a fascinating, if abbreviated, tour. There was far more in her laboratory than could be discovered in twelve short minutes. Nicholas doubted he could understand it all in twelve months or twelve years.

Miss Mitchell was nothing short of a genius. He loved listening to the passion in her voice as she described how the layer water between the nested containers of her *bain marie* allowed gentle heating at fixed temperatures, or the struggle to achieve the perfect drip rate and monitor appropriate volume levels without disrupting active experiments.

He drank it all in. He couldn't look away if he tried. Science made her so beautiful. Her eyes sparkled, her skin glowed, and her joyful smile could be felt all the way to his toes. He was forced to engage every shield in his arsenal.

She was exactly the wrong sort of woman. Not because of her interests or looks or mannerisms. But because he was going to miss her. His throat dried. He had never missed anyone before. Never known anyone for long enough. Every second spent with her would flay open his soul when it came time to leave.

And of course he would walk away. It was what he did. But more importantly, if she was wrong for him, he was very, very wrong for her. She knew it as well as he did.

All he had to offer was a body that she had helpfully pointed out would one day soon be going to shite, rendering him useless. What she had to offer was beauty and brains, science and sweetness, biscuits and friendship and laughter. She deserved more.

He wished he could impress her the way she impressed him. Their easy rapport was as terrifying as it was addictive. He enjoyed her company so much. Dreamt each night about coming back.

He thought again about the scrap of glass lying out on her mantel. It symbolized so much to him, although to any other observer it would look like nothing at all. Perhaps her maid would mistake it for rubbish and toss it directly in the bin. Perhaps she would do so herself.

After all, she didn't expect anything from him. To her, he was just some rake with nothing but wenching on his brain.

His stomach twisted. He could fix that, if he told her the truth. He could say *we both love creating things with our hands* or even *I have a workshop, too.* But what if she laughed? Or what if she believed him, but didn't care?

The only way to prove himself to her as something other than an aging gigolo would be to rip off the mask. He could not risk destroying the image he had so carefully crafted. It was all he had. Once it was gone, there would be nothing to fall back on.

A dull object crashed to the roof over their heads with a thud, followed by a strange, rhythmic scratching sound.

Her startled eyes met his. "Something's on my roof."

He nodded. "I hear it."

They listened for a moment in silence.

"What is it?" she whispered.

"No idea," he admitted. But perhaps this was a better way to show his usefulness. "Do you have a ladder?"

CHAPTER 8

*P*enelope stood in the center of her drawing room with one ear turned attentively toward the ceiling. Once the ladder was secured against the roof, Nicholas had ordered her back inside, so she would not catch cold. Nonsense, of course.

She could have argued that today was unseasonably warm. Or that the night they'd gazed up at the stars had been a half degree above freezing. But he wanted to handle the situation, and to be honest, it was lovely to have someone taking care of her.

Lovely in a terrifying sort of way.

She had never experienced anything like it. Never met anyone like him. Together, they formed a compound she was not quite able to identify.

To keep her mind off irrational matters like emotion, she glanced about the drawing room to see what might require tidying up.

Nothing, she realized with a sigh. Tidying up was what she did when she was trying to avoid uncomfortable thoughts in her mind, which was why her cottage stayed immaculately tidy.

A glint of sunlight from the front window refracted on a shiny surface atop the mantel. She hesitated. There should be no shiny surfaces atop her mantel. She moved closer to investigate.

It was a shard of glass. No, not a shard. A petal. It had been left there for her. Her stomach gave a little flip as she lifted it in her palm. This wasn't just any petal. It was a rose petal. One that would not be swept away by the wind or wilt and crumble into nothing.

She closed her fingers about the smooth, delicate glass and held it to her chest. Where on earth had Nicholas purchased such a perfect gift?

A frantic knock sounded upon her door. Penelope shoved the petal back upon the mantel and rushed to answer.

"You have a burglar," Virginia said, panting. "Someone is up on your roof."

Penelope dragged her inside and shut the door. "It's not a burglar. Saint Nick is up on the housetop."

Above them, footsteps paused, then began anew.

"You have a rake on your roof?" Virginia chuckled. "Isn't that a risky object to keep about?

Penelope was unamused. "What's wrong with being a rake?"

"What's good about it?" Virginia countered.

"It's honest," Penelope said without hesitation. "No promises or emotional manipulation. Men like Nicholas take extra care to ensure all parties not only know what they're getting, but get what they want. Come to think of it, he executes the role of rake rather scientifically."

Virginia's eyes widened. "You approve of the man you're interested in being a rake?"

"I'm not interested in him," Penelope protested. "I'm interested in science. Everything we do is an experiment."

"I thought a visit from Saint Nick was only supposed to be one night," Virginia said with a grin.

Penelope scowled at her. "He comes during the day."

"I imagined as much." Virginia tilted her head. "Have you fallen in love with him yet?"

"There is no love," Penelope said in exasperation. "So, no, I haven't fallen in it."

"Are you sure you don't believe in love?" Virginia asked. "Or is the problem that you believe other people aren't capable of loving you?"

"I..." Penelope glanced away. "Don't be ridiculous."

Blast Virginia and her razor-sharp questions. Penelope crossed her arms over her smock and wished she had something to tidy.

It had nothing to do with romance. Biologically speaking, of course, any member of any species would wish to be attractive to its own kind. If not to be loved, then to be chosen. Perhaps to come together in a reproductive ritual. Perhaps to form a more lasting mate bond. Those weren't emotions. It was nature.

A clatter sounded on the roof, followed by an extended silence.

Penelope and Virginia exchanged concerned glances.

Just when she couldn't stand the uncertainty any longer, the front door burst open and Nicholas strode inside bearing a wide grin and a small poof of fluffy brown feathers in his hands.

"You got a pet!" Virginia exclaimed in delight.

"It's not a pet." Penelope stepped closer to inspect the tiny chick shivering in Nicholas's hands. "This little thing made all that noise?"

He nodded. "I think it crashed into the chimney."

"You should name him Rudolph," Virginia suggested.

"No," Penelope said quickly.

"Randolph," Virginia tried again.

"No," Penelope repeated.

"I know," Virginia said slowly. "Name him 'Reindeer.'"

Penelope turned around. "It's a bird."

Virginia put her hands on her hips. "Have some whimsy."

"I could use some whiskey," Nicholas said. "Why are we naming the bird?"

"We're not." Penelope took another look at the trembling chick. "What's wrong with it?"

"Its wing is hurt," he said softly. "I'm afraid of making it worse."

Penelope glanced over her shoulder at Virginia. "Can you help it?"

Virginia's eyes narrowed as if sensing a trap.

"Please," Penelope coaxed. "I'll let you name it."

Virginia rushed forward to take the chick from Nicholas. "Dasher will be fine before you know it."

"Dasher?" Nicholas echoed.

"She dashed into your chimney," Virginia explained. "She's a chaffinch. You can tell by the white bars on her wings."

"Then she's in good hands," Nicholas said solemnly.

"The best," Virginia agreed. "I will get her situated at once."

She disappeared as quickly as she had come.

Laughing, Penelope turned to Nicholas.

He was standing right before her. Close enough to touch. Her heart lurched. She wanted to kiss him for a job well done. Throw her arms about his neck, and lay her ear to his chest to calm her racing pulse with the beat of his heart.

She did no such thing. It would spoil the experiment. *Duchess* was a test to see if Nicholas would throw himself at her, not the other way around.

"What were you doing while I was on the roof?" His eyes widened. "Wait. You're a natural philosopher. Were you transmuting lead into silver?"

"I'm a chemist, not an alchemist." Her lips quirked. "Besides, you were only gone for eighteen minutes."

He widened his eyes. "How long does transmutation take?"

"Three hours and forty-seven minutes," she told him with a twitch of her lips. "If you're a madman who believes in such things."

"Like James Price?" Nicholas cast his gaze skyward. "I was still in leading strings when he published that ludicrous claim about inventing a powder that turned mercury into gold, but even back then I knew he was a charlatan."

Penelope frowned. Nicholas read essays on alchemy?

"Price has his shortcomings," she admitted. "As does his acolyte, Josias Humphries."

"Humphries doesn't have shortcomings. He's a blithering idiot," Nicholas said with a groan. "Do you know what happens to iron at 2,800 degrees? It melts."

"I did know that," Penelope said. "Why do you know that?"

The wry humor vanished from his eyes. "I… Doesn't everyone know that?"

"Most people don't know the temperature at

which water boils, and it's a task they perform every day." She narrowed her eyes. "Do you melt iron every day?"

"I prefer to make tea out of water," he assured her. "Otherwise the leaves get all stuck. Have you ever tried to stir sugar into a glass of molten iron?"

"I don't imbibe more than the daily recommended dosage," she said with a straight face. "Now, confess. Why do you know about iron?"

"If you owned a carriage, you too could spend more time in a blacksmith's shop than actually driving. I'm thinking about getting a sleigh."

"I should've known," she said with a laugh. "Rakes have one interest, and it isn't science."

A shadow crossed his eyes. "I did pay attention to lectures. Does it surprise you?"

Did it? She supposed it should not. If she could be a woman and a spinster and a chemist, there was no reason he had to limit himself to being a single-minded rake.

"Did you get good marks?" she asked.

"The worst," he answered cheerfully. "Just to appease my father. He believed a man's interest should lie in women, not scholarly pursuits."

She arched a brow. "Were there many women at Eton?"

"Regrettably, it remains a school for boys." His blue gaze was intense. "You would have done very well there, I imagine. Been 'top prefect' in no time. The utterly obnoxious sort, with exemplary marks and perfect recall of every lecture."

She shook her head. "I like to think I would've been the one accidentally blowing up the chemistry laboratory."

He burst out laughing. "You'd like that? Is blowing up laboratories a particular dream of yours?"

"An occupational hazard," she corrected with a smile. "You've seen the metal door. Thick sheets of metal also span the interior of the walls all around the laboratory in case of fire. Even if it blows, the rest of the house should stay standing."

His brow furrowed. "But what about you? Is your smock some sort of anti-chemical, anti-fire material?"

"Oh, I would be incinerated with the rest of my equipment," she replied. "I'd be famous in no time."

"Please don't get famous," he said fervently. "I prefer seeing your molecules clumped together in their current form."

Her cheeks warmed. "Even my freckles?"

"Especially your freckles." His voice had grown hoarse.

Her stomach flipped.

"You do?" she whispered as he slowly lowered his head toward hers.

"I like these freckles." His lower lip brushed featherlight against her left cheekbone.

She shivered, her heart pounding.

"And I like these freckles…" His mouth brushed against the opposite cheek. "And…"

She held her breath, terrified she would vaporize from anticipation alone before she received her first kiss. "And what?"

"And I'm very interested in your mouth," he murmured huskily.

At last, his lips brushed hers.

Her pulse soared. Her breath caught. Her entire body surged with awareness.

She was going to swoon.

Heaven help her, she was going to embarrassingly and un-scientifically melt into a puddle of quivering Penelope molecules right at his feet. He was finally kissing her. His mouth was warm and sweet and perfect. She was frozen solid in shock.

Wait, no she wasn't. Her legs trembled quite alarmingly. And her arms—dear God, when had she wrapped them about his neck? How was she supposed to mentally tally every interaction when she could no longer think about anything but this kiss?

His arms wrapped warm and tight about her. His lips were gentle against hers. Even if she swooned, he would keep her safe. But she did not dare swoon. She did not want to miss a single moment of his lips kissing hers.

The heady sensation of her heart pressed against his did not calm her pulse, but sent it racing even faster.

She had to regain her senses. This was just

biology, she reminded herself urgently. The way her breasts grew sensitive and her nipples hardened, the desperate sensation of want deep in her core. It wasn't personal. This was how their species survived.

Kissing was a reflexive part of the human mating ritual, like the dance of the ostrich or the displays of the puffer-fish. It was nature, nothing more.

And yet, when his tongue touched hers, she was swept into another world. Their connection was not biology, but electricity. A lightning strike, again and again, anywhere their mouths or skin touched. It was the most dangerous storm she could have imagined. A hurricane of unprecedented feelings, overwhelming and unpredictable. A rush like nothing she had ever imagined. Something new that could only be achieved with him. Together.

"What am I doing?" he gasped, and reared back in obvious horror. "Miss Mitchell, please accept my deepest apologies. I—"

"Penelope," she whispered.

He ran a hand through his hair. "Penelope, I'm so sorry. This was… I have to go."

Before she could answer—if indeed she was capable of forming coherent thoughts—he swept his hat back onto his head and rushed out the door.

Penelope sagged against the closest wall and tried to catch her breath. Or her thoughts. At this point, regaining any sort of equilibrium would be a miracle. This afternoon had been a revelation.

He liked her freckles. He liked her mouth. He liked kissing her.

She closed her eyes and groaned. Devil take it, she liked him. It wasn't just an experiment. It had turned into something more. For her, anyway. For him... She brought her fingertips to her lips as if she could keep his kiss pressed there forever.

Foolish girl. She'd gotten what she wanted, hadn't she? The trial was over. *Duchess* worked. They were done.

No. She dropped her hand from her mouth and pressed her fists to the wall. It was a good start. *Duchess* might be working, but more evidence was needed.

Anyone could steal a kiss. No one purchased expensive perfumes for that. They wanted something more. They wanted everything. She could do no less.

The sexual act was an unequivocal criterion. A biological imperative. It was chemistry. Something she understood. Something *Duchess* ought to be able to help facilitate, if she was ever going to bring it to market. She could not give up field research now.

All in the name of science, she reminded herself firmly. Her sudden interest in participating in a mating ritual firsthand wasn't about her wants and desires. She wasn't falling for

Nicholas. She was simply performing thorough research. As a student of nature.

She lifted her wrist to her nose. The scent was light, but still there. Not that there had been any doubt. He had *kissed* her. She could still taste him on her lips.

Penelope gazed bleakly in the direction of her laboratory, unable to smile at her success. The better her perfume worked, the less she wished it would.

She wanted Nicholas's kisses to be real.

CHAPTER 9

"*T*hank you for meeting me," Nicholas said as he strode into the castle library.

"The wind does not meet the river, but flow together until they part," Miss Virginia Underwood replied thoughtfully.

Nicholas blinked. "Am I the wind or the river?"

"Dasher is no longer in my possession," she announced. "He is being cared for in the aviary, along with Dancer."

He tried to follow along. "Who is Dancer?"

"The partridge." She clasped her hands in joy. "The aviary population has doubled in size."

"The aviary's inventory has soared all the way up to two birds?" he asked. "That's... Congratulations."

She gave him a beatific smile. "How can I help you?"

Nicholas was beyond help, really. He could

not stop thinking about the kiss he'd shared with Penelope. It was only a kiss. How did he end up like this?

All of his previous liaisons had been with women with whom the scheduled activities were a foregone conclusion. There wasn't much else. Certainly no romantic kissing. And definitely no long conversations, or baking teams, or funny moments only the two of them understood.

He had no idea what to think about Penelope. Or what to think to do about any of it. So he had resolved to take his mind off her the only way he knew how. Return to his workshop.

What he needed was a new obsession. He'd rented the smithy for the rest of the week, and intended to lose himself in crafting a new mold. The more complicated, the better.

Although he doubted anything could be more complicated than the strange new emotions warring in his chest.

"They tell me you are an animal expert," he said.

Miss Underwood pursed her lips. "We all have passions."

"Do you know about turtles?" he asked quickly.

He didn't want to think about his passions. Turtles were a far safer topic. Their lives were simple, their shells complex. It would take intense concentration to design a mold with full accuracy. It was exactly the project he needed.

Miss Underwood's eyes grew wary. "Can anyone know turtles?"

"I don't mean their personalities." He pulled a small sketchbook from his pocket and opened to the most recent drawings. "I tried to capture as much detail as I could, but I'm relying mostly on memory. Is this turtle similar to the specimens local to Christmas?"

"Nothing is similar to that drawing." Miss Underwood wrinkled her nose. "It's an abomination."

"It is not an abomination." Nicholas straightened the sketchbook. "It's a turtle."

"Not any turtle known to man," she countered. "You've combined the retractable head of the Cryptodira with the larger carapace of the Pleurodira. And you've drawn the shell with fourteen scutes, which is either one or two scutes too many, depending on—"

His heart sang in relief as she listed her complaints. Turtles were complicated. He would have no time at all to think about Penelope. Researching the different shell contours and toe webbings would keep his mind more than occupied.

"What you meant to draw," Miss Underwood informed him, "are turtledoves."

"I absolutely meant to draw a turtle," he assured her.

"Because they come out of their shells?" she asked. "Noble and honorable creatures. But you meant to capture a turtledove. They mate for life."

"I'm not interested in mates," Nicholas said hastily. "Just a single, solitary turtle. One."

"Turtledoves," Miss Underwood repeated. *"Turr, turr."*

He stared at her. "What?"

"Turr, turr," she trilled, accompanying the coo with a gentle flap of her arms. "You may recognize the sound as the call of a turtledove seeking its mate."

"I'm not trying to learn its language," Nicholas said. "I'm trying to draw it."

"You should stop thinking of women like biscuits," she scolded him.

"What?" he choked out.

She crossed her arms. "You can't just eat one and then immediately go on to the next one."

"That is exactly how people eat biscuits," he said. "It is the only way. What does it have to do with anything?"

"Wait here." Miss Underwood made an about-face and disappeared amongst the stacks of books.

Before Nicholas could decide whether or not he was meant to follow, she reappeared with a slim volume in her hand. "Sketches from the Royal Ornithology Society. Turtledoves, pages eighty-eight to ninety-three."

He accepted the book. There was no other option. "Do I need to sign my name somewhere, or...?"

"Is your sketch for Penelope?" she asked.

"It is not for Penelope," he said quickly. "I doubt she's an aficionado of the genre. There are no *objets d'art* in her cottage."

Miss Underwood eyed him knowingly. "So when you enter her home, you know you are looking for something. You thought it was art. It is not."

"What is it I am searching for, O Wise One?" he said in exasperation.

She flapped her arms. *"Turr, turr."*

"You're wrong," he said firmly. "You have no idea what I'm doing. This project is for me. I'm not looking for anything else."

"But is Penelope?" Miss Underwood asked archly, then turned and walked out of the library.

Nicholas glared after her in consternation.

The only thing Penelope sought was a chemical combination for her new perfume. She was far too busy for anything else. Her life was full of interests and hobbies and activities. The baking and laboratory experiments alone gave her little time to be sitting around thinking about life, or turtledoves, or Nicholas. She wasn't the least bit clingy. A trait he respected in a woman.

Penelope had never once paid him an unexpected call, or begged him not to leave when his visits came to a close, or—

Good God. Nicholas snapped up straight in horror. *He* was the clingy one.

He hurried from the library. He had to get to the smithy, quick. Prove to himself he had plenty of better things to do than sit around reminiscing about a steamy kiss he'd shared with a lady chemist. He paused with his hand on the banister.

What if Penelope *would* consider mating for life? She might not believe in love, but she believed in nature. As a woman of science, she might very well select a biologically ideal candidate amongst the local gentlemen and wed him out of a sense of duty to the continued propagation of humankind.

Worse, she might find someone she *liked*. Someone truly perfect for her.

Nicholas's stomach turned. He didn't want her to fall for someone else. Nor could he see how such an eventuality could be prevented. Better gentlemen routinely offered things Nicholas had never considered. They were willing to promise an entire life, when Nicholas had only ever been willing to give a single night.

He forced his feet to continue their descent down the spiral stairs. It didn't matter. He was only here for a few more days. No need to complicate matters further.

Once he was gone, Penelope would forget him. And he... He would go back to the way things were. The way they'd always been.

Rather than lift his spirits, the realization made his chest feel empty.

He slid his hand into his pocket to ensure the

sketchbook was still there, nestled against the slim volume of ornithology.

Feathers were a thousand times more intricate than turtle shells. He'd design a partridge. It would take hours of concentration to blow glass delicately enough to do it any justice. He might not leave the smithy for the rest of the week.

When he reached the foot of the stair, he strode toward the castle exit.

He didn't make it.

Penelope was standing near the refreshment buffet.

His feet were already turned in her direction.

Her eyes brightened when she saw him. She gestured to the young lady at her side. "Nicholas, this is my friend Miss Godwin. Gloria, this is Mr. Nicholas Pringle."

Gloria, who believed in love.

The first conversation he'd had with Penelope came rushing back. *Duchess* was for women like this one. Penelope was a good friend.

He made an elegant leg. "The pleasure is mine."

Miss Godwin neither simpered nor curtsied. She glanced between him and Penelope, widened her eyes, and took an unsettled step back. "Lovely to meet you. I have to go. The waxing gibbous moon is… waxing."

She all but ran off, as if the cosmos required her immediate attention.

"I don't think your friend approves of me," he said dryly.

Penelope's expression grew wicked. "She may have mentioned that she finds your brother superior."

Nicholas brightened. "Did she?"

"Don't be offended," Penelope assured him. "Attraction is the result of a complex mixture of factors, including olfactory scents and receptors."

"I wasn't offended," Nicholas answered. "I am thrilled to hear Christopher's olfactory whatsits are superior to mine."

"Or it could be Gloria's receptors," Penelope said slowly. "I'd have to test to be sure. Did you become a rake due to environmental influences or your innate chemistry?"

"What?" he stammered. "Is that something you can test for?"

"I don't know." She tilted her head to scrutinize him. "It would be a fascinating study. How would you describe the formative impact of the male figures in your life during your childhood?"

"Look at the time," Nicholas said quickly. "I turn into a pumpkin every day at…"

Penelope glanced at the clock in the receiving hall. "Half four in the afternoon?"

"Precisely at half four," he agreed. "It's a common condition. Details are well-known. No need to do any studies."

"Drat," she said with a little sigh. "I do love studies."

That was part of what made her so dangerous.

He didn't want to expose his childhood or his emotions. If he were a turtle, he would have no intention of giving up his thick shell. He didn't even like to talk about last week, much less his past. Life was simpler that way.

But a woman like Penelope would never take *Sorry, I'm a turtle* as an excuse. An experimental chemist like her would want to investigate all his hidden facets. Poke him, prod him, until every secret he had ever held was hers to judge, and react as she would.

Nicholas could not think of a worse end to a relationship.

"Did I catch you entering the castle or leaving?" he asked to change the subject.

"Leaving." She held up a small notebook. "I was just making some quick tallies of this afternoon's biscuit distribution."

Nicholas had no idea what that meant, but he did like biscuits.

And Penelope.

A frisson slid over his skin as he realized just how much he really liked her. It gave her power over him. It made him vulnerable. He did not want to consider how he would feel to discover the feeling was not reciprocated. That he was nothing more than a test subject to be studied.

He swallowed the agonizing thought, and proffered his elbow. "May I see you home?"

"Thank you, kind sir." Penelope curled her fingers about his arm with a smile.

A sudden flap of wind fluttered his coattails as someone ran past, right behind them.

"*Turr, turr,*" came the gurgling coo.

Penelope startled. "What was that?"

"Nothing." He all but dragged her toward the door before she could glance behind him.

"Was that Virginia?" she asked.

"I think it was a bird." He changed his mind. "Or a madwoman."

"They should put her in charge of the aviary," Penelope said. "Perhaps she would meet a nice gentleman who shared her interests."

"I don't think a two-bird aviary requires more than one person in charge," he said dryly.

"I meant a gentleman customer." Her eyes widened. "Are there two birds now?"

"Miss Underwood donated Dasher." He led her around a small puddle. "Are there many clients, male or otherwise, who visit a one-bird aviary?"

"If there are," she admitted with a smile, "I am certain they would have plenty in common with Virginia."

Nicholas tried to imagine Miss Underwood presiding over a two-bird aviary, giving her unique style of lecture to a gentleman who had traveled there for expressly that purpose. He could not decide if a comedy or a tragedy would ensue.

"She is such a kind soul," Penelope said

softly. "She'd be the perfect candidate for *Duchess*."

"All men don't throw themselves at Miss Underwood's feet?" he teased.

Penelope frowned. "They should."

Nicholas tried to imagine a world in which England's most eligible bachelors were drawn to a remote village to swoon before Miss Underwood.

"God help us all," he muttered.

Penelope glanced up at the clouds. "I wonder if she'll ever marry."

He shrugged. "Does she want to?"

"Aren't all women supposed to want to?" she countered.

He paused. "Do *you* want to?"

"I've never wanted to." She glared at the horizon. "I don't see the point. Passion is chemistry. No other species complicates a perfectly natural act with dowries and courtships and boring sermons no one is listening to because their stomachs are growling."

"Is that all marriage is?" For some reason, the thought disappointed him. "Unnecessary pomp and circumstance tacked on to a purely biological coupling?"

He regretted the question as soon as it was out of his mouth. Why was he arguing against her? He wasn't trying to talk her into marriage. It would be beyond hypocritical to claim finding a bride as some sort of goal he had been working toward at any point in his life.

So why did it feel as though a knife twisted in his chest every time Penelope mentioned she had no need for love or passion or marriage? He should be glad. He'd be leaving soon. What she did or didn't do with her life after he was gone was none of his business.

But it *felt* like his business. It was all he could think about. Her lack of interest in a romance with him. The possibility of her changing her mind with someone else. Someone better. Someone… marriageable.

He tightened his jaw and forced himself to rein in his fears. They didn't matter. He had to stay emotionless. These moments with Penelope were nothing more than an unusually prolonged encounter. He should treat it as no different than any other meaningless rendezvous.

Perhaps they would come together in… Natural human nocturnal behavior. Perhaps they wouldn't. Either way, it would soon be over. If she wished for physical intimacy, he would be delighted to oblige but he knew better than to involve his heart.

"What is it like to have a brother?" she asked.

He glanced over at her. "You have no siblings?"

"Does it show?" Her expression turned curious. "Is Christopher also a rake?"

"Christopher is not a rake." He forced himself to ask. "Does it bother you that I was one?"

Am. Surely he'd meant *am*.

"Not at all," she said in surprise. "One cannot

fight one's nature. You're you. You should stay you."

His gut twisted. She had meant no insult, yet her easy acceptance felt more like a rebuke than a compliment.

Was being a rake truly his destiny? It might have become second nature over time, but that had been due to habit. If it was important for a man to be true to his essence, did he even know who that was?

Or was this another of her tests?

"You don't think there's anything wrong with being a rake?" he asked suspiciously.

She narrowed her eyes. "Do you think there's something wrong with being a spinster?"

"Do you think being a rake is like being a spinster?" he stammered.

She shrugged. "Both are happily unwed."

He arched his brows. "Are you certain all spinsters are happy to be unwed?"

"Are you certain all rakes prefer a life of solitude?" she countered.

He'd *thought* he was certain. Now he wasn't sure about anything.

"If I were to… not be a rake," he said carefully. "Would you like that better?"

"I would like you the same," she answered immediately. "I'd be interested in studying the variables that prompted such a change in behavior. But I would still find it in my heart to bake you biscuits."

She twinkled up at him.

He could not help but return her grin.

Penelope was unlike anyone he'd ever known. She didn't want him to fit any predetermined role. Not rake, not lover, not husband. She wanted to know him, not change him. *He* was the one who had begun to question his choices.

A crack of thunder sounded overhead.

They both lifted their heads to the sky in time for the first droplets of sleet to splash into their faces.

"It's coming," he said. He braced his muscles. "On your mark."

She gripped his arm tight. "Run!"

They tore off down the street, panting and laughing as the sky opened up and drenched them in cold rain.

By the time they arrived at Penelope's doorstep, they were both completely drenched, and their cheeks hurt from laughing.

"Coming inside?" she asked.

He shook his head. "I have an appointment across town."

"I'd tempt you with biscuits, but I've been so busy that I forgot to send my maid to market." She pushed a hunk of wet hair from her eyes. "I suppose I should get out of these damp clothes."

Nicholas imagined himself unrolling her stockings one by one, hanging them up by the mantel with care, then slowly unbuttoning her—

"Good plan," he said hoarsely.

Now that the overhang of her roof protected them from the rain, perhaps it was time to open his other coat pocket. The one without ornithology.

He shook the rain from his hand and pulled out a small, brown-paper package.

Her eyes widened. "What is—"

"It's nothing," he said quickly. "Open it later. When you're not busy."

"I will be stuck in my laboratory the next few days," she said with a sigh. "I've so much work to do."

He nodded. "I won't bother you."

"You can if you want," she said softly, then slipped inside her cottage and shut the door.

Nicholas raked a shaking hand through his soggy hair. Apparently, he'd lost his hat at some point and hadn't even noticed. All his attention had been on Penelope. He reached out to touch the knocker, then shoved his hands back into his pockets.

His whole life, he had limited far more than his interactions in an attempt to avoid becoming attached. He'd limited his hopes, his emotions, his happiness. Now look at him.

Clutching his coat, he turned from her door and stepped back out into the rain. His chest pounded. It was too late to stay safe.

He was in very, very deep trouble.

CHAPTER 10

*P*enelope carefully allowed a single drop of liquid to fall from one flask to another.

Duchess was nearly perfect. All she was adding now were flourishes. Floral notes above and beyond the underlying chemistry to mask science with sweetness. She inhaled the final aroma and smiled.

Ladies would try a perfume because it smelled nice. They would become repeat clients because it worked.

Since she'd begun testing *Duchess* herself, Penelope had noticed a distinct shift in her interactions with gentlemen in her community. Eye contact, where before there was none. Greetings that lasted longer than *how do you do*. Attention from a certain charming scoundrel she couldn't keep from her mind.

Everything about him was seductive.

She slid a glance to the package Nicholas had

given her the day before. It sat unopened next to her *bain marie* and notebook. A brown paper temptation, when she ought to be working. Her fingers twitched. She wasn't a silly, rake-obsessed chit like the ladies he was used to.

Of course she could wait to complete a respectable day's work before opening a simple gift. Besides, it wasn't as if she were expecting romance.

Penelope turned back to her flask and adjusted the flame. Maintaining the proper volume was so troublesome. She could measure a given amount of liquid into a tube, but wouldn't know with certainty how much had evaporated unless she stopped the experiment to measure, at which point—

An unbidden memory heated her cheeks. In a fit of extreme non-coquettishness, she had complained to Nicholas about that very subject just the other day. She set down her tools and buried her face in her hands. Was it any wonder the man had other things to do?

A choked laugh escaped her throat. Nicholas had no doubt stopped listening the moment he realized "flask" had nothing to do with whiskey. Literally any other woman in Christmas would show him a more interesting time. Penelope's idea of excitement was Dalton's argument for atomic theory based on measurable mass.

Well, that was the test, wasn't it? Not if she could catch a man using artifice and feminine wiles, but if she could maintain a rake's attention whilst being utterly herself.

With a little help from *Duchess*.

She stared in frustration at the orange flame flickering beneath the vial before her. A strange unrest filled her. Using science to incite a man's passions was all well and good. Indeed, before *Duchess*, she'd never incited more than a yawn.

But she had begun to want more than passion. More than biology. Her chest tightened. She wanted Nicholas to understand her. And like what he saw.

"Imbecile," she muttered under her breath. "Perfumes aren't magic."

She had to stay logical. Rational. Calm. Patient. Soon the trial would be over. He would return home; she would return to her laboratory. Who cared if—

Penelope snatched the package off the counter and sliced the cotton string binding it together.

She tried to calm her heart. The only reason Nicholas believed himself even cursorily attracted was due to an aromatic blend of chemical compounds. Not her personality. Any gifts he brought were therefore meaningless.

Her fingers trembled. What did she expect to find inside? Chocolates? An embarrassing flush heated her ears. Was that not what she wanted from him? To be wooed like any other woman, even if it wasn't real? Muscles tense, she unfolded the paper and pushed it aside.

Flasks.

Her breath caught.

He'd bought her *flasks*.

Her heart beat out of control. She lifted one of the delicate glass cylinders to inspect it.

It was the same as the model she normally purchased, save for a few key modifications. The lip was not completely round, but contained an external dip on one side, allowing the wielder to control the pour of liquid with greater precision.

The base was the same roundness, the body the same thickness, but tiny indicators on the glass would allow her to gauge the volume of liquid inside and whether its value had changed. The design was perfect.

She clutched all four flasks to her chest. He did see her. He did know her. He understood her. She couldn't stop smiling. This gift wasn't the traditional fare any gentleman purchased for any woman, but something meant specifically for *her*.

So where on earth was he? Since delivering the gift, he had disappeared. Her smile dipped at the edges.

He was not promised to her. A rake, by definition, did not promise himself to anyone. The gift might mean nothing.

Perhaps his natural wanderlust had led him to other women. Those who could be won with a single red rose. She swallowed a sour taste. The moment he exited *Duchess*'s scent range, she would no longer be foremost in his thoughts.

No matter. Science was the only thought she intended to keep in mind. Chemistry was the sole commitment she had time for. Anything else was an unnecessary complication.

She stared down at the flasks in her hands. Her shoulders curved. She would thank him for his thoughtful gift. He was a nice person. A temporary tourist who would soon return where he belonged. She placed the flasks back onto the table. There was no room in the equation for emotion.

She shouldn't make more of it than what it was.

A knock sounded from outside.

She blew out the candle and went to answer.

Before she could finish opening the door, Nicholas barreled in hefting a large wicker basket.

Her heart filled with joy. "What are you doing?"

He grinned at her. "I come bearing gifts."

"Frankincense, gold, and myrrh?" The corners of her mouth twitched.

"Close." He strode past her into the kitchen and dropped the basket on her table with a thud. "Flour, sugar, and butter."

"How *much* flour, sugar, and butter?" she asked suspiciously. "That basket looks like it weighs two stone."

"I panicked." His eyes were impish. "Running out of biscuits is like running out of…"

"Oxygen?" she guessed.

He shook his head. "Hot chocolate."

"Humans can live very long lives with no consumption of chocolate," she informed him gently.

"But without chocolate, are we truly living?" He shot a stern glance over his shoulder before continuing to unload the basket. "I think that's everything. I added each ingredient to my list when we made the last batch."

"You did? I didn't see you write anything down."

"Mental list," he clarified. "I'm almost as good at list-keeping as I am at biscuit-eating."

He was right. Everything she needed was there.

"You purchased all of this because I chanced to mention I hadn't had time to go to market?"

He nodded. "Confession: after long and careful consideration, I concluded that your lack of biscuit ingredients was at least partially my fault."

"Very self-aware," she murmured. "But that was yesterday. What if I've been to market in the meantime?"

"Then we'll have even more biscuits." His eyes brightened. "Did you?"

"No." She stifled a giggle at his crestfallen expression.

"You are a cruel, cruel woman," he chastised

her. "I shall write your name on the 'wicked' list for teasing me."

"It's not teasing," she protested. "I'm a natural philosopher. Science deals with hypotheticals."

"And I will deal with *you* later." He gathered her measuring cups and a mixing bowl, then pointed toward the stools. "Sit. Allow me to demonstrate the only chemistry lesson I ever paid attention to."

Penelope selected the closest stool and rested her elbows on the counter behind her in order to watch as he worked. Her insides felt warm and her normally tight muscles were unusually relaxed.

This was what it felt like to have someone take care of her, she realized. No—not to take care of her. To care *about* her. A delicious shiver skated across her skin. She hadn't just crossed his mind. He had acted on his feelings. She couldn't stop smiling.

She did her best to focus on the recipe. "Make sure the eggs—"

"No interruptions, Natural Philosopher," he scolded her. "Your kitchen is not my first workshop. Science is about observation, is it not? Your job is to observe silently."

She tried to keep a straight face. "What if, in the name of science, I happen to observe that you look especially fine today?"

He gestured with his fingers. "More detail, please."

She affected a dry, scientific tone. "One

might observe that the tailoring of today's coat emphasizes the strength of your muscles. That the gold in your waistcoat brings an extra sparkle to your eyes. Or how the smudge of flour on your left eyebrow makes an unusual sartorial touch."

"You may comment upon your uncontrollable attraction to me at will," he assured her. "Do continue. What were you saying about how the sight of me sets your loins a-quiver?"

She burst out laughing. "I didn't—"

"How gravely you wound me, madam." He sent her a faux petulant glare. "Just as I was debating sharing these biscuits with you."

She clutched her hands to her chest in shock. "Who is this imposter in my kitchen? The real Saint Nick would never voluntarily share biscuits."

"I was tricking you," he agreed. "The biscuits are for me. Your gift is the empty basket."

"It's a lovely basket," she said solemnly. "It smells of wicker and unrealized potential."

"There might be a single portion of fine chocolate inside," he said. "Also only for me."

She grinned and hopped off the stool to investigate. There was indeed fine chocolate inside. More than enough for two. He'd thought of everything.

Her heart gave a little flip as she surveyed the kitchen. As much as she loved the pretty stone, the glass petal, the incredible flasks... His other presents had been static objects meant to be enjoyed by her alone. Today's gift was an experience meant to be shared together.

She could not think of anything more romantic. But it was all thanks to *Duchess*.

After a quick taste of the batter, he slid the first tray of biscuits into the oven and grimaced. "As much as it pains me to say this… Can you set that abominable alarm?"

"As you wish." She started the kitchen chronometer and then positioned herself directly before him. "I've only one question. How ever will we pass twelve long minutes?"

He moved closer, sending her a sultry glance from beneath his lashes. "Mmm. I doubt your suggestion at all resembles my—"

She twined her arms about his neck and pressed her lips to his before he could continue.

He immediately enveloped her in his warm embrace and returned her kiss with passion. She felt her heart melting. He tasted of sugar and nutmeg and long, cozy nights. Each kiss was a promise of something more, something better. He did not want to change her into someone she was not. He wanted to bring her pleasure, exactly as she was. And she absolutely intended to let him. Starting with—

The experiment, she reminded herself with a start. This was a trial for *Duchess*, not a fantasy for Penelope. She'd almost ruined it by kissing him, instead of waiting for him to kiss her.

It was too late to stop now. But to keep the results pure, she could not allow herself to be the aggressor, even in something as simple as a kiss. If their physical interactions were to progress further, he would need to instigate each step from his own free will.

Please let there be additional physical interactions, she begged the fragrant drops of perfume on her pulse points. His every kiss incited a whirlpool of emotion, a surge of desire so intense it took her breath away. And when his tongue touched hers…

Every molecule of her body wanted this man more than she'd dreamed possible. It was as if she was hydrogen and he was carbon and together their irresistible chemical bond had joined to form ethylene, a substance so flammable that any spark could cause it to combust.

At this rate, her entire kitchen was going to ignite.

Each delicious, drugging kiss caused an instant reaction of subsequent sparks from her mouth to her core. Her pulse raced for him. Her body begged for him. Her—

He lifted her waist and swung her onto the edge of the table. Her heart pounded in excitement. The sudden arrival of her derrière knocked one of the eggs off the other side of the table and to the floor.

Penelope did not care a button about broken eggs or melting butter or the puff of flour that her skirts had sent flying. From this angle, her hips were now at the same height as Nicholas's, aligning their sexual organs perfectly.

She couldn't wait to find out what he intended to do about it.

Without breaking their kiss, he slid his hands over the curve of her hips, up the dip in her waist, coming to rest so close to her bodice that the edge of his fingers brushed against the curve of her breasts.

Her nipples immediately responded. The pad of his thumb stroked the side of her breast. She held her breath. Her skin tightened in anticipation, yearning for a touch that did not come.

He lifted his lips a fraction from hers. "May I—"

"Yes," she gasped. "Immediately."

His mouth once again claimed hers.

Slowly, inexorably, his hand at last cupped her breast. Her entire body came alive at the touch. His fingers teased her nipple lightly, devastatingly, flooding the pleasure regions in her brain with a strong urge to rip her clothes from her body in order to give him greater access. To give him anything he wanted.

She couldn't say so aloud. All she could do was respond to his kiss.

He hiked the hems of her skirts up just high enough to allow his hips to nestle between her thighs. Her breath caught. Even though several layers of clothing still separated them, there was no mistaking the hardness pressing against her core.

Experimentally, she rubbed against him.

He gasped into her mouth and grabbed her hips tight. "Good God, woman."

"I liked it," she whispered against his lips. She should not have done that. "Should I stop?"

"I like it, too." His voice was scratchy and tortured. "Do it again."

As his kisses once again robbed her of thought, she gave up on tally-marks for the experiment. This was so much better. His talented hands caressed her breasts, her trembling legs were locked tight about his hips, and the throbbing of—

A deafening clamor rent the air as the mechanical alarm sent hundreds of nails pounding against sheets of metal.

He leaped back and glanced wildly about the kitchen in desperate search for the switch. "Where do I...? How can we...?"

She slid from the table and raced to the switch, sliding perilously on a patch of runny egg in the process. Her hand slapped at the control until the racket finally stopped.

Unfortunately, so had their intimate moment.

"I should've set it for twelve hours," she muttered.

His eyes twinkled. "I don't know what you've heard... but the middle eight hours would probably be me sleeping."

She leaned forward with interest. "And the other four hours?"

"Spent exactly how you think," he responded

at once, unrepentant wickedness glinting in his eyes. "Toss me a towel?"

She handed him her wool-lined baking mitts, still reeling from their kiss… and the idea of experiencing far more for hours.

He pulled the tray out of the oven and set it on the cooling cloth in the middle of the table.

"Should I start the chocolate?" she asked. Her voice was surprisingly steady, but her trembling legs threatened to melt into a puddle at his feet at any moment.

"The chocolate is for you." He stepped close and lifted her hand as if to kiss it, then turned it over to press a soft kiss to her wrist instead. "You smell delicious."

"It's the biscuits," she blurted. But she deserved the awkward reminder.

It wasn't the biscuits. It was *Duchess*, rudely reminding her that Nicholas was simply responding to biological urges she'd chemically engineered for precisely this purpose. Her stomach twisted.

She wished she was worse at chemistry. That his extremely pleasing reaction was to *her*, not to a complex blend of compounds and extractions. That she had never started this trial at all.

He straightened his jacket and gave her a crooked smile. "Thank you for a lovely afternoon."

"You aren't staying for biscuits?" Her heart gave a lurch of disappointment.

He paused. "Is that what you want?"

"Are we… still talking about biscuits?" she stammered.

"We should figure that out," he said, his gaze intense. "And possibly allot ourselves more than twelve minutes."

"But you're a rake," she babbled. For a man famed for his conquests, Nicholas was proceeding remarkably slow. Curse her inability to instigate properly! "What is there to figure out? This is what you do."

"Wrong," he said, his voice rough. "You are not 'what I do.' This is something else entirely. Something I'm not certain either of us is ready for."

She hesitated. "Because I'm a virgin and you're not?"

"Perhaps there's more than one way to be a virgin," he said at last. His brow furrowed as he ran a hand through his hair. "I'm always ready for a tumble. I've never had it mean something before."

Her heart stopped. "What does it mean?"

His intense gaze focused on hers. "That continuing down this path would be dangerous."

And with that, he was gone.

CHAPTER 11

*N*icholas warmed the tip of his blowpipe in the fire. The simple, calming act should have made him relax. Made him feel at peace with the world and himself.

It did not.

He clenched his jaw. Although this rented space did not fully replicate his workshop back home, the smithy was not the cause of Nicholas's unrest. A certain tempting chemist was. She had haunted his thoughts since the moment he walked out of her home.

Perhaps he *should* have stayed for biscuits. He shoved the tip of his blowpipe into molten glass. No. He should not stay for biscuits. There were no biscuits. There was only hot, sweaty love-making, which was especially odd phrasing, given he had never made love to anyone before. His liaisons had just been meaningless tumbles.

Not that he was in *love*. He wasn't that foolish. This was a mere infatuation. His first. No wonder it was so confusing.

Every moment with Penelope was like being with... what? A friend? A lover? Something in-between?

That was the problem. He had friends and he'd had lovers, but he'd never had an "in-between" before. It marked a perilous crossroads. Friends were forever. Lovers were temporary. If Penelope crossed from one side to the other...

He whirled the molten glass onto the end of his blowpipe. Being afraid of losing Penelope was ridiculous. Walking away had always been the plan. He was on holiday, not some bride-hunting expedition like his brother.

Not that Penelope was the sort to seek empty promises or try to change him. Was that what stung? That there was no ambiguity?

She had clearly been open to full physical intimacy. The reason was clearly because he was a rake, therefore loving and leaving was "what he did." And he clearly should have taken her up on the offer because great Zeus, he could not concentrate on blowing glass into a mold.

What had he been hoping for? That *she* would fall in love with *him*? He snorted. That would also be a first.

He slumped forward and rubbed his temples with one hand. She expected things from him. All the wrong things.

Or perhaps logical things, and he was the

one who had changed. He didn't want his old life anymore. He wanted something better.

He wanted *her*.

Nicholas broke the blowpipe from the clay. There he went again. He had planned to craft a turtle. Or a pheasant. Anything would do, as long as it had nothing to do with Penelope.

Of course, that was not what happened. Even as he'd fashioned this mold, he'd known its glass figurine wasn't for him, but for her.

It would get locked in his cupboard with all the others just the same.

He shoved the clay mold aside and began to pace the workshop. He despised not knowing what to do. Penelope wanted a liaison with a rake. Nicholas happened to be a rake. An obvious solution presented itself.

Except he didn't *want* to be a rake. Had unconsciously stopped the same day he met her. Now that they'd spent so much time together, he had thought she'd seen something more in him than a caricature.

He had been wrong.

Wanting a true connection, dreaming of "love" like an utter lunatic, those things weren't for him. He'd learned long ago not to reach for what he wasn't meant to have.

He had to go back to what he knew. Penelope wanted one night with a rake? He would give it to her. It would have to be enough for both of them.

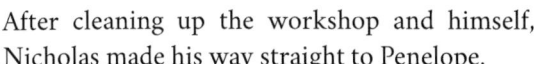

After cleaning up the workshop and himself, Nicholas made his way straight to Penelope.

"One night?" he demanded.

His heart pounded. For the first time, he had arrived empty-handed. Today he had nothing to give but himself.

She peered up at him. "What?"

"One night?" he repeated, his voice cracking. "That's what you want?"

A frown marred her brow. "Isn't it what *you* want?"

"Yes or no." He jerked a hand through his hair in nervousness. "We can be intimate, or we can leave things as they are. I need to know before I come inside."

She bit her lip. "You'll come inside either way?"

There was his answer. He gave a crooked smile. "I'm satisfied with a simple plate of biscuits."

"I'm not." Her cheeks flushed pink, but she didn't look away. "I want it all."

Even better. He swung her into the house, kicked the door shut behind them, and covered her mouth with his.

Her lips were warm, and familiar, and welcoming. Returning to her arms was like coming home. A cozy fire, protected from all the snow. He could not help but deepen the kiss.

She smelled heavenly, and she tasted like…

cinnamon sugar? His pulse jumped. He fervently hoped the kitchen alarm wasn't about to sound.

He lifted his mouth from hers. "Are you baking?"

"I was." Her lips curved as she gestured behind him. "I set your biscuits out by the chimney. Do you want to start with a snack?"

"I do not." Yet he made no attempt to drag her to the closest horizontal surface. He needed to make certain they both understood what they were agreeing to. "I'm here on holiday."

She nodded. "I know."

"A fortnight," he clarified. He wished he could stay longer, but he had given his word to his brother. Chris deserved the chance to bridehunt without Nicholas's presence getting in his way. He let out his breath. "My holiday will be over in two days."

She nodded again. "And then you return home."

"Yes." He gazed into her eyes, willing her to understand. "At present, I have no plans to come back to Christmas."

She tilted her head in confusion. "I know all that. What does it have to do with tonight?"

"I…" His mouth dried.

Blast it, his logical chemist understood perfectly. *He* was the dreamer.

"It has nothing to do with tonight," he admitted. He lifted her chin with his knuckle and brushed his lips over hers. "Tonight is about us."

"You smell different." She nuzzled closer, as though to breathe in his aroma. "I like it."

He couldn't help but laugh. "It's not a perfume. I smell like…"

His laughter cut off with a start. Had he really been about to say, "a blacksmith?" Was he *mad?*

He was heir presumptive to a dukedom. Society's most celebrated scoundrel. The only thing a man like him was expected to do with his hands was to—

"You smell like what?" she prompted, her wide brown eyes gazing up at him.

His heart stuttered. He'd come here to make love to her, not to lie to her. If puncturing the bubble of his "dashing rake" persona made him no longer of interest because it spoiled the fantasy…

At least she would know who he truly was.

"The smithy." He cleared his throat. "I smell like a smithy. I've been renting it to use as a workshop."

She seemed to think this over. "Your hobby is… blacksmithing?"

"Art," he said hesitantly. "I know it's foolish mummery, but—"

"The petal," she breathed. "You made the petal?"

The back of his neck heated. He hadn't expected her to guess what it was, much less that he'd made it by hand. He gave a short nod.

"It's not mummery, you daft man." She put

her hands to his chest and pushed him aside. "It's beautiful. Even prettier than the rock you gave me. You're very talented."

He watched, immobile, as she crossed to the mantel. First, to inspect the stone that had reminded him of her eyes, and then the glass petal.

"This rose petal is perfection. Delicate and strong." She turned it over in her hand. "I can't believe the papers don't give as much ink to your art as they do to your bedsport."

Nicholas was glad of it. He had gone to great lengths to keep the secret.

She glanced up when he didn't answer. Her eyes widened in shock. "They don't know?"

"Nobody knows." He rubbed the back of his neck. "Except Chris. And now you."

"Nobody knows?" she repeated in disbelief. "Why doesn't anybody know?"

Because Father's lack of patience for unmanly behaviors had resulted in some of the worst moments of Nicholas's childhood. The harsh punishments for each infraction had caused art to intertwine with self-recrimination until he could no longer separate the two.

"Just a lad trying to make his father proud," he muttered.

Her brow furrowed. "With art?"

"Without it." Nicholas cleared his throat. He hated discussing private embarrassments. "Father felt it wasn't manly."

Penelope stared at him as if he'd lost his mind. "But art *isn't* manly."

His stomach hollowed in shame and guilt. "I know. That's… literally what Father always said."

"Was he a man of science?" she demanded. "Because I am a student of the genre, and I find his conclusions lacking."

Nicholas blinked. "What?"

"Art isn't manly or womanly or anything else. It's *humanly*." She frowned in thought. "I haven't done enough research to determine if other animals display a similar trait."

"What?" he repeated blankly.

"Facts. I can name hundreds of 'manly' artists," she continued. "Titian married his housekeeper after she gave him two sons. When Rembrandt's wife took ill, he took her nurse as his lover. If by 'manly' you mean 'shameless roués.' I shall refrain from listing the countless men who painted erotic nudes of their paramours to keep them warm on lonely nights, or I won't cease talking all evening."

"You know about art?" he stammered.

"The artifacts on display at the Egyptian Hall in London made me curious about the chemical progression of paint composition over the centuries, which led me to—" She snapped her teeth closed and took his hands firmly in hers. "Nicholas. I regret to inform you that your sire was a blithering idiot."

He stared back at her speechlessly. What if she was right? His heart pounded. What if she

141

was wrong, and unmasking his true passions earned him nothing but scorn and humiliation?

She bit her lip. "I'm sorry. Too direct?"

"Your mind may be scientific," he said at last. "But other people—"

"The opinions of strangers are irrelevant. Live for yourself." She squeezed his hands. *"Be* yourself. All they'll have is gossip. You'll have *art."*

Vertigo assailed him. Tonight he would have something even more precious than art. He would have Penelope.

He pulled her into his arms and kissed her from somewhere deep in his soul. A secret place he'd been hiding his entire life. She'd seen through his defenses, torn away his shell, and *liked* what she found.

With her, he was not some empty Lothario, but an artist. Which meant tonight, he could come to her not as a rake, but as a man.

As himself.

He slid his fingers into her hair as he kissed her. *She* was the work of art. He savored the softness of her skin, the sweetness of her scent, and the heat of her mouth. Yet her kisses were more than just Eden for his senses.

Touching her was no mindless diversion, but a startling bond that grabbed his heart and refused to let go.

The thought of an emotional connection terrified him. His pulse would not stop racing. Wild thoughts slashed through him like lightning strikes. Kissing her was a perfect storm of pleasure and vulnerability and desire.

But with her, he didn't want some forgettable encounter. He wanted to cherish this night for the rest of his life. No matter how much it scared him.

"One night?" he murmured between kisses. "You're certain?"

She grinned up at him. "This very night, if you're so inclined."

"I'm actually here for two more days." He kissed each corner of her smile. "I can make room in my schedule for a second visit."

She twined her arms about his neck. "Let's start with tonight."

A lead weight punched into his gut.

Not a yes.

His first time asking to prolong a liaison. The first woman with whom he could not begin to guess how many nights together could ever be enough. And she did not feel the same. *Yet*, he reminded himself.

The evening was not over. He would make it perfect.

He swung her up into his arms and kissed her with everything he'd been holding back.

"Bed?" he gasped, when he came up for air.

"Too far." She gestured behind them, panting. "Chaise longue. Much closer."

He would have preferred a bedchamber. More romantic, more special, more... *official*. But the evening wasn't about him. It was about

Penelope. Anything she wanted, he would give her.

In less than a heartbeat, they were reclined on the chaise and back in each other's arms. His pulse galloped in urgency. Perhaps it was their proximity to the fire that simmered his blood and fogged his brain.

Or perhaps it was the knowledge that this might be their last night. Their *only* night, if he didn't do this right. He cradled her face and kissed her.

"Touch me," she whispered. "Like you did before."

With pleasure.

That was, until a belated thought struck him.

"The alarm isn't set, is it?" he asked suspiciously. He loved the taste of spiced sugar but did not look forward to falling off the chaise in a blind panic. "How much time do we have?"

Her gorgeous brown eyes twinkled up at him. "Is sunrise long enough?"

He gave her a lopsided smile. He rather suspected a thousand sunrises wouldn't be enough.

CHAPTER 12

*P*enelope's heart raced in anticipation of Nicholas's touch. Although she now knew how intimate her breast would feel in his hand, the decadent sensation still took her breath away when at last he gave her the delicious torture she sought.

His kisses were just as magical. Heady and disorienting, full of wicked promise and incredible sweetness. She wanted it all.

When he broke their kiss, she raised her head to complain—until he tugged down her bodice and placed his mouth to her breast. With a gasp, her head fell back against the cushion to revel in the sensation.

Had she thought his fingers were delicious torture? This was a hundred times worse and a thousand times better. It defied science. It was pure feeling, pure desire. Her body didn't just yearn for the sex act. She yearned for *him*.

Nicholas was the active ingredient in this

combustible formula. His kisses made her light-headed because *he* was the one doing the kissing. His touch made her desperate for more because it was him that she wanted.

He saw her as more than some bluestocking spinster. More than a science-obsessed lady chemist. He saw her as a passionate, sensual woman who was all those things and so much more. Worthy of his desire, and her own. She threaded her fingers into his hair.

He, too, was far more complex than appeared at first glance.

Although she did not know art as well as chemistry, she understood wanting to make new things with one's hands. She happened to do so in a laboratory, and he with a kiln. They were more alike than one might think. It frightened her.

Any woman with a pulse would beg for a chance to share physical pleasure with a man like Nicholas. The realization that they might form a compatible compound made her glad he was going away. She could not stand to have him close, and still not *have* him.

But for a few hours, he was hers.

Her back arched with pleasure at his touch. She could not wait to copulate with him. He was all she could think about.

Today, she wore extra droplets of *Duchess* on each pulse point. Everything else could come off. She'd happily burn her clothes in the fire to bring her body in closer contact with Nicholas.

He was magnificent. The sensations his mouth teased from her nipples made her want—

Cool air kissed her bare thighs as his warm hand slid to cup her core. Her mind fogged. When had he lifted her skirts? Were they even still clothed? She didn't know and didn't care. He'd begun to dip a fingertip inside. Rhythmically. Deliciously.

He returned his mouth to hers as he continued to work his magic.

Her lungs forgot how to breathe as the inexorable coil of want began to expand and build within her. She recognized the warning signs. Her fingers were not nearly as talented as his but had often brought release she could not find elsewhere.

He was bringing her close to the edge, but she didn't want his fingers. She wanted him. All of him. This was a moment that was meant to be shared.

She tugged his shirt from his waistband, fumbled for the buttons of his fall.

He lifted his lips a breath above hers. "What are you doing?"

"Trying to free your sex organ," she panted. His fingers had not ceased their ministrations and it was becoming increasingly difficult to form coherent words. "I want it inside of me."

He paused. "What did you just say?"

"I want your sex organ inside me right now," she repeated, then hesitated. "Is the suggestion unclear?"

"Very clear," he assured her, and claimed her mouth in a long kiss. "And a splendid idea. My sex organ thinks your idea is the best suggestion it's ever heard. I was just thinking that before we get to that step, I might pleasure you in a few other ways first. Specifically, I could—"

"You could stop talking." She grabbed the sides of his face and pulled his mouth back down to hers. "You might also—"

"Take your suggestion." He lifted his hips and unbuttoned his fall without delay.

She knew the precise moment because the heat and weight of his shaft now pressed just inside her thigh. Her pulse skipped. They were closer, but not close enough.

She'd waited her entire life for this. She now realized she'd been waiting for *him*. It was time. She could not bear a moment more. Not when every molecule of her body yearned for him. Her hands ran over his hard muscles. She longed to combust together. Didn't he?

Her heart pounded uncertainly. "Aren't you—"

"I'm getting there." He took a ragged breath. "Penelope, I've never… There might be pain." His words were husky, his gaze agonized. "I'm so sorry. The last thing I want to do is hurt you."

She shook her head. "You won't. I'm ready."

Very ready. His fingers had already brought her close to her peak. There might be some pain upon entry, but not much. After all, there was no barrier for him to breach. She'd taken care of that years ago with an accidental discovery.

Since long before the ancient Greeks, women had been using artificial phalluses to pleasure themselves. Evidence could be found in paintings and antiquities collections all over the world.

After investigating the evolution of methods and varieties, what woman of science could resist the professional obligation to perform empirical personal research?

As enjoyable as artificial phalluses turned out to be, the experience would be nothing like this one. Penetration substitutes were sturdy, but lifeless. Meant to be used in solitary circumstances.

Or were they? A scandalous experiment flashed through her mind. What if she were to wield her false phallus, whilst Nicholas—

All thoughts of future erotic experiments vanished as he nestled his very real phallus at her entrance. She wrapped her legs about his hips and gasped at the sensation. It was not pain at all, but a thick delicious fullness. A connection unlike any other.

This was perfect. *He* was perfect. Hot and hard, sensual and strong, carnal and caring… She cupped his face and kissed him with a fervor she could not control. Their chemistry was magical.

That their union should occur on the chaise before the fire was even more perfect. She'd chosen the drawing room on purpose. Here, where they always exchanged their gifts. The pretty stone upon the mantel, the glass petal, the plates of fresh biscuits… and now each other.

Her spine arched with pleasure. The wet friction of each stroke, the sweet heat of each kiss—nothing could stop the chemical reaction building between them. At any moment, the explosion would happen.

She gripped her legs tighter about him, matching him stroke for stroke. "Nicholas, I think I'm going to…"

"Don't hold back," he murmured between kisses. "I'll join you."

She couldn't hold back if she tried. The knowledge that they were about to reach their peak together pushed her over the edge. Release flooded her. She cried out as dizzying waves of pleasure took her higher than she had ever been. All because of him.

She thought she detected complementary throbbing begin in his phallus, but after one final pump he jerked free from her embrace, bucked his hips beneath a handkerchief, and collapsed back on top of her.

Progeny. He'd had the presence of mind to prevent potential progeny. She swallowed hard.

Thank heavens one of them had behaved rationally.

A woman of science would never admit being swept away by illogical emotions. Next thing you knew, she'd claim to believe in miracles and true love. Nonsense. She brushed a damp curl from Nicholas's forehead and tried to calm her pulse.

"One night to slake our lust," he mumbled. "Do you feel well and truly slaked?"

The corners of her mouth twitched. "If I say no, will you do it again?"

"We'll do it even better," he promised sleepily. "You skipped a lot of good bits."

Her heart thumped. "I might like that. After you wake up."

"I might stay just like this forever," he murmured, and nestled close. "I love the way you smell."

At his words, cold sliced through her heart. He hadn't made a connection with *her*. His instincts had responded to a chemical compound. She stopped stroking his hair and tried to blink the hot stinging from her eyes instead. He was here in response to her *scent*. Exactly as she manufactured it.

She hated *Duchess* a little more every day.

Her throat tightened. She'd wanted this moment to be true. But it wasn't. None of this was real. This was an illusion of intimacy engineered in her laboratory, with no regard for his feelings on the matter or her own. She deserved exactly what she got.

Even if that meant nothing at all.

CHAPTER 13

*P*enelope wrapped her scarf tighter about her neck. She was standing in the makeshift observatory at the rear of Gloria's cottage, but the open window was not the source of her cold. Penelope's emptiness came from within.

Gloria glanced up from her telescope, her gaze concerned. "Are you ready to talk?"

"No."

There was nothing to discuss. That was why Penelope had ushered Nicholas out the door as soon he had re-buttoned his fall, washed off every trace of perfume, and buried herself alone in her bed with only her thoughts and the darkness of the night to accompany her.

Gloria gave her a sympathetic look. "Then why are you at my house before dawn?"

"I knew you'd be awake," Penelope answered immediately. "You stay up all night to watch the stars."

"I know why I'm awake." Gloria narrowed her eyes. "Why are *you* awake?"

Because no matter how far Penelope hid beneath her blankets, sleep had refused to come. She had gravely miscalculated the aftereffects of *Duchess* achieving a successful trial.

She did not feel as though she'd won. She feared she had lost much more than her virginity. She had lost her focus. Her rationality. She needed to get it back.

Gloria turned back to her telescope. "I stopped by the castle for supper last night."

"Hm," Penelope responded distantly. "Anyone there?"

"Only every female in Christmas," Gloria said with a laugh. "The dining hall has been overflowing with women for two weeks. Every lady in there is hoping to catch sight of—or spend the night with—Saint Nick."

Penelope's stomach filled with nausea. She longed to ask if Nicholas had been present to bask in the adoration, but she dreaded the answer. Either way, if he had not returned to the castle after leaving her cottage, that meant he had gone somewhere else. Possibly to someone else. And if so, she didn't want to know.

"Trust me," Gloria said with a roll of her eyes. "If *Duchess* was ready for sale, you could make a fortune in the next half hour."

The knife in Penelope's stomach gave another twist. *Duchess* was ready. Penelope was not. She certainly did not want other women using it on Nicholas.

The thought of him engaged in intimate activities with someone else... White-hot jealousy roiled her stomach. Based on observable history and empirical patterns, a rake engaging in consensual copulation with everyone he pleased was not a hypothetical situation but a foregone certainty.

Gloria angled her head. "What's wrong? You used to find such antics amusing."

Had she? Penelope wrapped her arms about her aching chest. Apparently, she used to be an idiot.

"You can't possibly be jealous," Gloria scoffed. "The moment you met him, you could not think of a worse sort of man. After you argued over *Duke*, I was certain that would be the end of it. Did you see him again after that time at the refreshment buffet?"

Penelope focused her gaze at the wall as though she no longer spoke English.

"You *did* see him again," Gloria breathed. "Good heavens, this isn't envy. This is possessiveness."

"I do not possess him." Penelope's voice cracked.

"No one could," Gloria agreed. "Luckily, it's not as if you two..."

Penelope pretended to be deaf.

"Did you?" Gloria demanded, hands on her hips.

Penelope wished she were invisible.

"You *did*." Gloria's eyes widened in disbelief. "When? How?"

Penelope sighed. "First…"

"Don't tell me," Gloria interrupted quickly. "I understand the mechanics. I just don't understand how they happened between the two of you. I thought you disliked him."

"I thought so, too." Penelope hugged herself tighter. "For a day or two. And then I…"

"And then you what?" Gloria arched a brow. "You thought the best way to settle your differences was to get naked and let biology take over?"

"Turns out," Penelope said, "that's a terrible way to settle anything."

"Good to know." Gloria stepped closer, her tone soft. "Then why did you do it?"

"I didn't mean to, at first. It was supposed to be a simple test. I wanted to prove that passion and emotion were illogical human behaviors, and that chemistry was not only more dependable, but more powerful."

"And now?" Gloria prompted when Penelope didn't continue.

She sighed. "Emotion is definitely illogical, and passion is as powerful as chemistry."

Gloria crossed her arms. "Did you truly believe women of science were exempt from emotion?"

"It's illogical," Penelope repeated. "I thought women of science were logical."

"You can be a chemist and aware of your emotions."

Penelope shook her head. "No one wants an emotional chemist."

"You mean, Saint Nick doesn't?" Gloria asked softly.

"He's not attracted to *me*," Penelope said. "I manipulated his brain into a false attraction to a chemical compound on my wrists."

"Dynasties have been built on less," Gloria assured her. "But what is your excuse? If he is a mindless gnat drawn to your honey-like wrists, what made you attracted to him?"

"Gnats aren't drawn to honey," Penelope mumbled. "Most feed on plants, although there are some carnivorous varieties that—"

"Penelope." Gloria sent her a warning look.

She let out a long, slow breath.

"He's kind," she said at last. "He's charming and handsome, yes, but so much more than that. He's… complex."

Gloria blinked. "Saint Nick, London's favorite rake, is complex?"

Penelope nodded. "I'm beginning to suspect everyone is. Until I met him, I thought I was simple, too."

Nicholas was more than just skillful in the bedchamber. He was funny, he was sweet, he was thoughtful. He was also a talented artisan.

Especially given the damage his father had caused, she respected Nicholas's commitment to art. Aware his peers would judge him or change their opinions about him if the truth were to come out, Nicholas hid that facet of himself, but he did not stop. He held nothing from his passions.

"No wonder everyone swoons over him," Gloria said.

"I wish I could swoon," Penelope said. "Lying unconscious would be preferable to my current state. All this emotion is overwhelming. I have no control over it. It's something that can only be experienced, not quantified. It's terrifying. I don't know what to do."

"Because he's a rake?" Gloria asked.

"Because he makes me feel like there's more to life," Penelope admitted.

Gloria cocked her head. "Like what?"

"Like… believing in love."

"Believing?" Gloria lay a hand on Penelope's arm. "You *are* in love."

Penelope's stomach bottomed. Bloody hell. This was not the result she'd been looking for.

"That's your hypothesis," she stammered.

Gloria was undeterred. "Are you afraid he doesn't feel the same about you?"

"I know he doesn't."

That was the part that hurt. Her perfume had worked. It made a man as amazing as him believe he was interested in her.

Unbeknownst to him, it wasn't true. It was just science. Carefully constructed aromas designed to fool his brain. Chemistry. Alchemy. Manipulation.

And Penelope was the one who had fallen for it.

"Why don't you tell him how you feel?" Gloria asked softly.

Penelope scoffed. "What would that do?"

Gloria pursed her lips. "You don't believe in reformed rakes?"

"No," Penelope answered bluntly. "Even if I did, I wouldn't want to change him. That's not what love is."

Gloria arched her brows. "Now you're an expert on love?"

Penelope was pretty sure she no longer considered herself an expert in anything. But if she found it objectionable for others to demand Nicholas give up his art, she could not ask him to forsake any other passions. Even the ones that made her want to cry.

"Do *you* believe in reformed rakes?" she countered.

"He's *ton*," Gloria admitted. "Isn't keeping mistresses acceptable Society behavior, as long as it's discreet? I am certain he wouldn't flaunt his other lovers in front of you—"

"He wouldn't have to. The caricaturists and the society papers flaunt all his indiscretions for him. I don't want the image in my head at all." Penelope rubbed her temples. "He's leaving tomorrow. That is the best thing for both of us."

Gloria crossed her arms. "What about love?"

"He's not in love," Penelope said in exasperation. "Once he is out of scent range, the effects of the perfume will wear off and he'll forget me completely. Life will return to normal."

"*His* life," maybe," Gloria said doubtfully. "What about yours?"

Penelope touched her fingertips to Gloria's telescope stand. "You have the stars. I have science to keep me busy. I'll be in my laboratory."

With the door shut tight to ensure she be unable to hear anyone knock. If she saw Nicholas again, she would have to confess the truth about the trial. She could not continue living a lie.

Gloria hesitated. "You plan to lock yourself in your laboratory until he's gone?"

"No," Penelope said. "That would be an ineffectual half measure."

She planned to cocoon herself in her laboratory for the rest of her life.

CHAPTER 14

*N*icholas shoved his blowpipe into the fire and glared at the dancing orange flames. Normally, nothing was as calming as blowing glass or crafting an intricate mold. This morning, he was far from calm. He had bolloxed things with Penelope.

He had wanted their first lovemaking to be perfect. Slow, gentle, romantic. Instead it had been fast and carnal. They hadn't paused to kick their shoes off, much less get undressed. And as soon as it was over, they were done. Goodbye.

For a rake, that specific sequence of events was often considered an ideal encounter. It was not what Nicholas had wanted to give Penelope at all. He wasn't certain how he felt to discover that it was all she had wanted from him.

Oh, very well, he knew exactly how he felt.

Miserable.

He gathered molten glass onto the tip of his blowpipe and sighed.

Penelope was marvelous. Smart and sensual, funny and logical. A scientist and a surprise. Any man would be lucky to have her. Nicholas preferred that the man in question... be him. But he couldn't blame her for turning him away.

What had he offered her? Not one night, but two? How generous of him. Imbecile. She should have made him exit through the chimney.

He locked the molten glass inside the clay mold and began to blow. It was all his lungs were good for. What could he have said to Penelope? The more he opened up, the more he risked being found not good enough.

As a rake, he was more than serviceable. He was splendid. London knew what to expect, and Saint Nick delivered.

As Nicholas the bachelor glassblower, however, he became an oddity. A hobby that would raise no eyebrows for a man outside the *beau monde* would make Nicholas a laughingstock.

He would not offer Penelope a laughingstock. Nor had he any intention of forcing her to mix with his fast London crowd. Not that it mattered. He had already been dismissed.

He snapped his blowpipe from the clay mold. Was he cleaving to the persona of Saint Nick for Penelope's sake, or for his own safety? Just because something was easy didn't mean it was right. Or good.

Devil take it, he didn't want two nights with

this woman. He wanted *all* the nights. Now unto infinity.

He dropped his head into his hands and groaned. He was in love, damn it all. And he only had two days left in Christmas. Time was disappearing fast.

He was going to have to tell her.

His legs shook as he jumped from the stool. Declaring himself to a woman was possibly the most terrifying undertaking he had ever attempted in his life, but Penelope was worth it. His heart thumped. They were a good match. She had to feel it, too.

He retrieved two molds from a hidden shelf. This was his gift. He had made them for her, and this was the perfect moment to deliver them. He cracked open the molds and carefully withdrew two glass figurines.

Turtledoves. One-of-a-kind, just like Penelope. Delicate to the eye. Stronger than they looked. The perfect gift to bring when informing a woman that one had fallen in love with her.

He hoped.

His muscles twitched. He'd never been in such a position. No one had ever loved him, chosen him, wanted him to stay. He knew not to expect too much.

But Penelope was worth the risk. What they were building was real. Not some temporary distraction, but a relationship based on mutual respect, honesty, and the sheer joy of each oth-

KISS OF A DUKE

er's company. Only a fool would walk away without trying to make it last.

He set the birds down just long enough to put the smithy to rights, then started for the road.

To label himself nervous would be a gross understatement. Penelope was clever. If she returned his affection, he would be vindicated. If she didn't... Then he supposed he really was the shallow, otherwise useless rake he had always pretended to be.

He tilted the top of his head into the wind and strode faster. The one thing that scared him more than rejection was missing the opportunity to try.

She was stepping onto her front stoop just as he turned up her walk.

His insides warmed, and an involuntary smile curved his lips. The sight of her always made him happy. He could not fathom where she might have been at this hour of the morning.

He caught up with her as she was about to shut the door.

She did not move aside. Or invite him in. Or smile.

"You said one night," she stammered. "It's daytime."

Not the most auspicious start. He pressed on anyway.

"Here," he said. "I made these for you."

Her hands seemed to accept his offering reflexively, rather than out of any particular desire to receive a gift. She did not even glance down to see what it was. "Nicholas—"

"They're turtledoves," he blurted out. So much for his grand romantic gesture. It could not possibly go worse, and he was powerless to solve it. Or stop his mouth from babbling. "Glass figurines. They stand alone, and they can interlock. Turtledoves mate for life."

Splendid. Now he sounded like Virginia.

To his horror, Penelope's beautiful brown eyes took on a wet sheen. Not in a *this-is-so-romantic-I-could-just-cry* sort of way, but in a *this-is-so-horrible-I-could-just-die* sort of way. "Nicholas—"

"I love you," he announced, using his last scraps of courage. "That's what I came to say. Even if you don't feel the same, I thought you should know."

"It's not love," she said, her eyes tortured. "It wasn't supposed to be like this."

He tried his best to hide the tornado of disappointment within. There was his answer.

He was not what she wanted.

"Very well," he said despite the swaying in his head. "There's no need to ask why. I can well imagine."

"I don't think you can. You don't know the whole truth." She took a deep breath. "It was me. Rather, it was *Duchess*. I believed I had perfected a formula that could manipulate male emotion—"

"You what?" he stammered.

"—but I couldn't be certain until I proved it. I needed a test subject in order to run the trials—"

"A what?" he repeated, taking a jerking step backwards.

"—and I gave the trial a strict time limit in which to accomplish predetermined tasks." Her voice cracked as she met his eyes. "The experiment worked beyond my wildest dreams."

"It *worked?*" he repeated, banging a trembling fist to his chest in anger. "You toyed with my heart to prove a theory?"

"That wasn't the intended goal." Her voice cracked. "I only meant to—"

"I was listening," he said, not bothering to hide his bitterness. "Your intent was to manipulate my emotions in order to trick me into playing the lovesick swain for your own amusement."

"Not amusement," she said quickly. "Science—"

He scoffed. "You are very amused by science. Don't shift the blame." His hands shook. "I believed you of all people would treat others with unfailing honesty, and you purposefully misled me."

"I…" She closed her eyes. "Yes. I did."

"It was a game to you." His heart lurched in humiliation. "See how long it took me to exhibit whatever behaviors you've been marking behind my back with your little tally marks."

She winced.

"I'm surprised you didn't enter your wager in

the betting book at White's," he said, each word scratchy and raw. "Then everyone could laugh at the silly laboratory specimen who believed he had finally unlocked his cage."

She shook her head, cheeks pale. "I never thought of you as a specimen."

"Didn't you?" His voice was empty. "Wasn't that how you chose me to be an unwitting part of your little experiment? You saw me as a *thing* instead of a person."

He had been such a fool. He'd believed he had found love, but he hadn't even found a real connection. He was just a research subject. An animal, like any other. Useful for a brief moment, then dumped back in the wild.

It had been a farce all along.

He should have known better. Of course she didn't love him back. Back when she'd selected him for a laboratory experiment, the one true thing she had told him was that she didn't believe in love. His useless heart banged against his ribs.

It didn't matter how real the past fortnight felt to him. To her… it wasn't. This was nothing more than the successful conclusion of a routine perfume trial. His chest tightened. She could skip back to her laboratory and concoct another potion, but he was done being part of her tests.

"I don't love you, then," he said hollowly. "As it happens, I don't even know you."

He spun around on stiff legs and strode as fast as he could from her door.

CHAPTER 15

*P*enelope hurried off her front stoop after Nicholas, but he was already heading back out in the street. Her chest ached at the damage she'd caused. He had deserved to know the truth, but she hadn't meant to hurt him.

"Wait," she called out. "Nicholas, please stop! Where are you going?"

"To fetch my belongings," he said without turning around. "I'm done here."

He did not slow down.

She forced herself not to chase him. She had no right to. Although she knew her own feelings were real, his interest had been caused by chemical compounds designed to manipulate him.

His affection was a mirage, no matter how much Penelope might wish otherwise. He had deserved to know the truth. She just hadn't expected it to hurt this much.

In one single moment, Penelope had destroyed everything. The haunted look in his eyes when she'd told him it was all a farce...

Her heart had broken along with his. She swore under her breath. *Duchess* had caused nothing but damage.

No. Penelope had achieved it herself.

She loved Nicholas, yet she had used him and hurt him. She deserved to lose him.

Penelope trudged back out into the street, not to chase him to the castle, but to allow him free will. She turned her leaden feet in the opposite direction.

Gloria's maid answered her door and allowed Penelope back inside without question. Less than an hour had passed. It felt as though she had spent it in a hell of her own making.

Penelope plodded into the observatory on heavy limbs and stood out of the way of the telescope. She hadn't come to talk. She just didn't want to be alone right now. Her home was too full of memory of Nicholas. Back when he thought he loved her.

Gloria was cleaning her telescope with a cotton rag. "I thought you were going to stay in your laboratory for the rest of your life."

"My life is over," Penelope said wearily. "Thanks to me."

Gloria turned from the telescope and squinted in Penelope's direction. "What are you carrying?"

"Turtledoves." Penelope clutched them to her chest. "They stand alone but fit together."

Gloria's eyes widened. "May I see?"

Penelope forced herself to relinquish the precious figurines.

"These are incredible." Gloria's eyes lit with wonder. "What an ingenious way to interlock the two. Where did you buy them? I want a pair, too."

Of course she would. The only thing Gloria loved more than the stars were mechanical puzzles. When the heavens were too cloudy for sky gazing, she spent long hours with her grand orrery, a mechanical device rotating a model of all eight planets. Gloria claimed she used it to unlock the mysteries in the sky.

Unfortunately, Penelope could offer no puzzle to solve. Everything was devastatingly, humiliatingly clear.

"The doves were a gift from Nicholas." Right before she'd informed him he was an unwilling participant in a chemistry experiment. She was surprised he hadn't taken them back and smashed them.

Gloria set down her cleaning rag. "If you still refuse to believe in love because 'it's not visible to the naked eye,' I'd say these doves are indisputably tangible evidence."

"I made a mistake." Penelope's shoulders slumped. "*Duchess* inflated my confidence, and I used misplaced pride to cause nothing but harm."

"'Misplaced' is right." Gloria put a hand on her hip. "Your perfume didn't help your confidence at all. Your only faith was in chemical compounds, when you should have had it in yourself."

"I am now incredibly confident in my ability to destroy the best thing that ever happened to me," Penelope assured her. "I interrupted a declaration of love to tell him it wasn't real. Now he's gone."

"Do you remember why you two argued when you first met?" Gloria asked after a moment. "What did you tell me?"

"That Saint Nick was on a mission to stop *Duke*," Penelope said with a bitter smile. She'd been so sanctimonious. "That the gallant rake feared confused, hapless women would find themselves leg-shackled to all the wrong men."

Gloria crossed her arms. "And what did you say to that argument?"

Penelope sighed. "I told him women aren't hapless. *Duke* starts the conversation. Women decide where it goes."

"Listen close," Gloria said. "Men aren't hapless either. He chose you. Not your scent. The whole package."

Hope pricked Penelope's heart. Might it be true? Could *Duchess* have worked as designed, yet not have manipulated the final outcome?

"You have to trust," Gloria said softly. "Have faith that what you feel is right. All sorts of non-verifiable things exist. If a rake can choose love, surely a lady chemist is capable of the same."

"I want to believe more than anything," Penelope whispered. "But it would truly be a miracle. The chemical compounds used in *Duchess*—"

"Are you wearing it?" Gloria asked, coming closer.

Penelope took a step backward. "What?"

"Are you wearing it right now?" Gloria sniffed behind Penelope's ears. "You don't smell like anything but Penelope."

Penelope pushed her away. "I washed it off as soon as I realized it had been a mistake. The trial is over. I'll never wear perfume again."

"When did you get rid of it?" Gloria insisted. "Did you pause to have a quick wash-up between accepting his gift and breaking his heart?"

"Of course not," Penelope said, exasperated. "If you must have every detail, I scrubbed it off last night before curling into a ball and failing to sleep."

Gloria grinned. "Then you weren't wearing it."

"What?" Penelope stammered.

"You weren't contaminated with your evil perfume." Gloria lifted her chin in triumph. "When he declared himself to you, *Duchess* was out of smell range. You were talking to the real Nicholas."

Penelope sniffed both wrists, then stared at Gloria.

"*Duchess* started the conversation," Gloria reminded her. "You had the power to finish it."

The power to ruin it, rather.

"It happened too fast. This was my first kiss, my first sexual encounter, my first—"

"Your first time glancing up from your notes," Gloria put in dryly. "You never came out of your laboratory. Not completely. Eligible gentlemen could leer at you all day long and you wouldn't notice. Until *Duchess* gave you a reason to start."

That… sounded uncomfortably accurate.

Penelope had done everything in her power to block herself off from the outside world. She hadn't realized just how well she had succeeded.

"He said he doesn't love me." Penelope's chest tightened with shame. "That he didn't know me at all. He's already gone."

Her heart cracked. She'd managed to realize both her worst fears at once.

Love was real.

And she'd lost it.

CHAPTER 16

*N*icholas attempted to enter his guest chamber without being spotted. In his current mood, he had no wish to converse with anyone, much less pretend to feel carefree and flirtatious.

Unfortunately, the door to his brother's chamber across the corridor was ajar, and Nicholas's arrival did not go unnoticed.

Before Nicholas even had a chance to ring for a footman to load his trunks into his carriage, Chris was standing in the doorway.

"Have you been to the roof of the castle?" he asked. "I have to fix my telescope. The view is astonishing."

"I'm leaving," Nicholas said. There was no sense keeping it from his brother. Nicholas's accelerated departure worked out in Chris's favor.

His brother frowned. "You have until tomorrow. Why would you leave early? This village is positively brimming with comely young ladies."

"I don't care about them," Nicholas muttered.

His brother stepped into the room and lowered his voice. "Is it the lady chemist?"

Nicholas did not respond.

His brother's mouth fell open. "Never say you've developed an infatuation!"

"It doesn't matter what I feel." Nicholas shrugged. "She was never interested in a lasting relationship. I was a convenient subject upon which to test the efficacy of her new perfume."

Chris raised his brows. "How exactly did the lady test you?"

Nicholas glared back at him stonily.

"Let me see if I understand." Chris came closer, stroking his chin as if deep in thought. "The individual in question slept with a willing partner, on precisely one occasion, with no inclination or promise, spoken or otherwise, to continue interaction after the deed was done?"

Nicholas crossed his arms.

"You got raked and don't like it." Chris's eyes lit with mirth. "She 'Saint Penelope'ed you."

Sometimes, Nicholas wanted nothing more than to throttle his brother.

"You cannot possibly be angry with her over it," Chris said in disbelief. "Do unto others, and all that. Weren't you always worried that someday a woman would agree to one night and not really mean it? Penelope meant it. Huzzah."

"It's worse than that. One night was what I wanted, too." Nicholas sighed. "Until I didn't."

Chris stared at him for a long moment, all humor gone. "You fell in *love?*"

Nicholas shrugged. "She didn't. So, it doesn't matter."

Chris stepped forward, his initial humor now replaced by wonder. "Good God. I never thought you'd fall before me."

"I never thought I'd fall at all." Nicholas scowled. "The landing is hell."

Chris reached out. "Nick, I'm sorry. Do you want me to—"

"No." Nicholas clenched his jaw tight and turned away before his brother could touch him.

He didn't want Chris's pity. He wanted to be as far away as possible.

It wasn't the village of Christmas he was running from, but stacks of warm biscuits placed by the fire. Afternoons side-by-side on stools in her laboratory or in the kitchen. Laughing at private jokes. Their hands touching as they kneaded a bowl of dough. Heated kisses that tasted of spice and sugar. The scent of her skin. The softness of her hair.

The finality in her tone when she admitted his time with her had been a test trial that had now concluded. She didn't need him anymore.

"Where will you go?" his brother asked, his voice concerned. "Home?"

"My workshop," Nicholas answered.

"What about London?" his brother insisted. "Parties. Dancing. Other women."

Nicholas shook his head. "You warned me

one day I would become too old to be a rake, and now that day is here."

"I said that two weeks ago," Chris pointed out. "You've barely aged a fortnight. I understand that rejection hurts. You don't have to be a rake, but you're too young to become a hermit."

Nicholas lifted his head with interest. "What is the minimum age? I hear the Weld family constructed a lovely hermitage on their country pile."

"You shall not take a post as a garden hermit," Chris said firmly. "You do realize the position requires you not just to live alone, but to avoid all contact with others."

"Exactly." Nicholas nodded. "The answer to a prayer."

All that awaited him in London was some new series of meaningless affairs. It was no longer what he wanted. He wasn't certain it had ever been something he desired.

He now suspected he'd been searching all this time for someone who would want more, someone he'd be unable to live without.

Playing the part of rake helped save his pride. He could convince himself that the emptiness in his life wasn't because he was unworthy of love, but because he had not yet met the right woman.

Well, now they'd met. And he was still unworthy of love.

Chest tight, Nicholas stalked to his dressing room and yanked the bell pull. "As soon as my trunks are packed, I'm gone. There's no reason to stay."

"Isn't there?"

Of course Chris would think that. He still believed in *happy ever after*.

"No," Nicholas said flatly. "It's over. If Penelope doesn't even want a two-night liaison, she's not going to marry me."

His brother raised his brows. "Did you ask her to marry you?"

"What would that have done?" Nicholas asked wearily.

Chris lifted a shoulder. "Why don't you find out?"

Nicholas scoffed. "No woman wants to marry a rake."

"You just said you weren't a rake anymore," Chris pointed out. "Marry her."

"I was a test subject in an experiment." Nicholas enunciated each word.

"You said that was over, too."

Nicholas clenched his fists, throat stinging. "I am…"

"All out of excuses?" his brother suggested.

"Hurt," Nicholas admitted in a low voice. "I tried to be honest and forthcoming in all my interactions. She let me believe we were creating something that didn't exist. I'm better off alone."

CHAPTER 17

*P*enelope was still slumped against the frigid wall in her best friend's private observatory. She stared across the telescope at Gloria.

"What are you looking for?" she asked at last.

"Answers." Gloria lifted her gaze from the eyepiece. "What are you looking for?"

Penelope cast her gaze down at the interlocking glass figurines cradled in her arms. "Impossible things."

If she hadn't created *Duke*, Nicholas would never have approached her. If she hadn't decided to experiment with *Duchess*, none of the past two weeks would have happened. She had lost him for the same reason that she had found him.

"You don't believe in impossible things." Gloria returned her gaze to the lens before her. "Which means whatever you're thinking about must still be possible."

"It's not," Penelope said. She had been dishonest. He wouldn't forgive that.

Gloria shot her a knowing look. "How do you know if you don't experiment?"

Penelope lowered her head in thought. If what had attracted Nicholas's attention was also what had caused her to lose it, could the same work in reverse? The original experiment had been about what Penelope wanted. What did Nicholas want?

Observation, she reminded herself. What were the observable facts? He never spent more than one night with a single woman. He had spent a night with Penelope. Ergo, he wanted her body. He had come back again. Ergo, one night wasn't all he wanted.

More facts. He designed superior measuring flasks for her. Ergo, he supported her interest in chemistry. He hand-delivered biscuit ingredients in order to bake for her. Ergo, he wanted to take care of her. To spend time together. He designed her the sort of bird that mates for life. And he said…

"He loves me?" she asked in a small voice.

Gloria's gaze softened. "Did he use those words?"

Penelope nodded.

"Then he does." Gloria's eyes shone with satisfaction. "What are you going to do about it?"

Penelope's stomach turned. "He also said he didn't love me anymore."

"And one of those statements was true," Gloria agreed. "Which one do you believe?"

A fortnight ago, Penelope did not believe in love. Today, there was nothing she wanted more.

She just needed to convince Nicholas.

Up until now, he had always come to Penelope. It was past time for her to go to him. Or at least try her damnedest.

It might be too late.

She rushed from Gloria's house without another word. She had taken too long already. The castle was enormous, but the staff was swift. They could have trunks packed and carriages ready in the wink of an eye.

Penelope raced up the snow-packed road toward the castle. If she did not catch him in time, she would lose more than her chance at a second trial. She didn't even have an address to send him a letter. If she couldn't find him, there wouldn't be another opportunity.

She dashed in through the castle's front doors and made her way past the reception buffet to the head housekeeper.

"Mrs. Blair," she gasped, her lungs burning from racing up the steep hill.

The housekeeper smiled. "How can I help you, Miss Mitchell?"

Penelope took a deep breath. "Which guest chamber belongs to Nicholas Pringle?"

The housekeeper folded her arms across her ample bosom and gave Penelope a disapproving stare. "Just like I tell all the other ladies. The day after the party, milord gave me explicit instructions not to share that information with anyone."

Penelope's heart skipped. "He did?"

That was the same day Nicholas had first come to visit Penelope.

The housekeeper harrumphed. "And I won't be making an exception for you. Marlowe Castle respects our guests' privacy."

A perfectly reasonable stance, and impossible to argue with. What next?

Penelope spun from the housekeeper in frustration and darted a panicked glance about the reception chamber.

Nicholas was nowhere to be seen, of course. He didn't want biscuits and spiced wine. He wanted to be far away from a woman he believed didn't love him.

"What are those?" came a dreamy voice from over Penelope's shoulder.

She jumped and jerked around, clutching the glass figurines to her chest for safety. "Virginia! I didn't see you. These are birds."

"Turtledoves," Virginia corrected, a self-satisfied smile spreading across her face. "Of course they are."

Penelope waved Virginia's cryptic comment away impatiently. Time was running out. "You live here. Do you know which guest chamber belongs to Nicholas?"

"Sixth floor," Virginia answered without hesitation. "South wing, left side, fourth door. Did you know that the nuptial flight of the European turtledove is often—"

"Thank you," Penelope called over her shoulder as she fled the reception area and dashed up the spiral stairs.

She could swear she heard Virginia trilling *turr, turr* after her as she ran.

Penelope flew up the stairs. Even though it might already be too late, even though love was scary and unknowable, even though she might have already broken things past all repair, she had to try. Nothing else mattered. She skidded off the landing and into the corridor.

The door to his guest chamber was open. Shadows moved inside. Nicholas might still be here!

She burst inside, out of breath and half wild. *"I love you!"*

Christopher Pringle stared back at her, eyes wide. His startled gaze dropped to the figurines. "Did Nick make those?"

"Er, not you." Penelope hugged the turtle-doves closer to her chest. "I meant—"

Nicholas stepped out from his dressing room, his eyes dark and unreadable. "*Out.*"

"Does he mean you or me?" Penelope whispered to his brother.

"Definitely me," Christopher said cheerfully. He slipped past her into the corridor, shutting the door as he left.

"I love you," she said again, her heart racing.

"People 'of science' perform experiments on animals," Nicholas said. "You don't fall in love with them."

"I'm not proud that I set out to manipulate you," Penelope admitted. "It was wrong of me. To be honest, I didn't believe it possible."

"Congratulations," he said icily. "Now you know."

Penelope bit her lip. "You don't understand. The experiment was whether I could attract a man as myself. We might have begun on false pretenses, but every moment we shared was you being you and me being me. Nothing could be more real."

He arched a brow. "Nothing?"

"You met the true me. You know the true me. You made love to the true me." She took a half step forward. "I'm so sorry I hurt you in the process. I was foolish. I don't deserve your forgiveness."

He let out a slow breath. "Penelope—"

"I won't sell it," she said quickly. "*Duchess* is dead. I'll stop *Duke*, too. I never expected a perfume to become my greatest achievement, and when I saw what it could do, my only thought was to give women the same advantages. I never meant to bring heartache."

"Perfumes can't break hearts," he reminded her. "Women who manipulate men into falling in love with them, despite having no interest in keeping them, break hearts."

"There's nothing I want *more* than to keep—" Penelope's voice caught. "You still love me?"

He cocked his head. "You want to keep me?"

"Of course I want to keep you," she choked out. "The experiment was to attract your attention, nothing more. I changed it to flirtation, in order to have another day with you. And then I changed it to a kiss, in order to have another. And then I changed it to—"

"Last night... wasn't part of the experiment?"

"The trial was successful on the first day," she admitted. "I couldn't give up the experiment because it meant giving up you. I thought the only reason you kept coming by was because the chemical scent engineered for my pulse points had bewitched you."

"Many things about you bewitched me." His lips quirked. "The chemicals behind your ears, however..."

"It's science," she babbled. "I could never have attracted you on my own. You can't deny it. *Duchess* was the one—"

"My turn," he said, and took a step forward. "You're right. I knocked on your door because I wanted to halt *Duke*, not seduce its creator. But that changed."

She nodded. "The 'one night' rule. I know."

"You don't know because I didn't tell you." His gaze was intense. "I realized I didn't want a night with you. I wanted all the nights. All the days. All the sunsets, and twilights, and sunrises..."

She bit her lip uncertainly, her throat scratchy. "You did?"

"No." He took another step forward. "I do. I always will."

"Me too," she whispered and threw herself into his arms. "I want you every single second. You are the reason I know love is real."

"You love me?" he whispered into her hair.

"With everything I have." She hiccupped into his cravat. "I love you more than alchemy and chemistry and biscuits—"

"Bad news," he told her. "I never said I loved you more than biscuits."

She slapped his chest and gazed up at him with hope in her heart. "I love you, Nicholas Pringle."

"I love you, Penelope Mitchell." His eyes twinkled. "Even more than biscuits. Will you be my wife?"

"*Yes.*" She pressed her mouth to his and kissed him.

The door swung open. "Your trunks are in the carriage, milord. What shall I tell the driver?"

Penelope's eyes met Nicholas's. "My house?"

"Your cottage contains a shockingly insufficient quantity of workshops," Nicholas said with a straight face.

The footman cleared his throat. "You're staying, milord?"

"I'm definitely staying." Nicholas tossed the footman a sovereign for his troubles and returned his mouth to Penelope's. "Banns take three weeks. Think we can build something more appropriate in that amount of time?"

CHAPTER 18

"*A*re you ready?" Nicholas gazed down at his beautiful bride.

Penelope grinned back up at him. "For anything."

She lifted her fingers to his elbow.

He swung her up into his arms instead. "Allow me to carry you across the threshold and into our new life."

Penelope's eyes twinkled up at him. "Does it count as new if we're going to be doing the same things as before?"

"Newer and better," he assured her. "Now we'll be doing the same old things together."

He turned toward the open door. Although the reading of the banns only required three weeks to complete, construction had taken months.

Their splendid fireproof home boasted what Nicholas considered to be not one, but three workshops. A chemical laboratory for Penelope.

A glassblowing and mold-making workshop for Nicholas. And a well-stocked kitchen for endless supplies of biscuits.

Not to mention an oversized chaise longue reclining beside their new chimney, just waiting to be christened.

Heart full, Nicholas stepped over the threshold with his wife in his arms. He swung her in a circle, then paused when he noticed the empty mantel. "Blast. I should have brought you a gift."

"You are my gift." She tilted her head towards the cozy chaise. "But if you really want to give me something..."

Their bodies entwined atop the plush surface in no time.

"Welcome home," he murmured between kisses.

Her eyes held a naughty glint. "I can't wait to spend the rest of my nights with Saint Nick."

"And your days," he said firmly. "Allow me to demonstrate what I have in mind."

They wouldn't leave their cottage for a week.

EPILOGUE

For the second time in Penelope's life, the castle ballroom brimmed with merry villagers. All her neighbors once again gathered under one roof to celebrate a perfume of her creation.

But this time, she hadn't done it alone. Nicholas was by her side, and had worked with her to make *Duchess* a runaway success.

"Can you believe this is happening?" she whispered.

He squeezed her hand. "You did this."

"*We* did this," she corrected him with a smile. "I cannot tell if demand is due to my perfume or the gorgeous bottles it's sold in."

Nicholas had changed his turtledove design from figurines to decorative perfume bottles. The intricate, delicate construction of the interlocking glass birds had more than doubled the price.

Cost didn't seem to matter. Clients who previously would have selected one or the other, now purchased *Duke* and *Duchess* together in order to own the collection.

"Speech, speech!" cried the crowd.

"What do you plan to say?" Nicholas asked.

"I'll start with the chemical composition of civet excretions," Penelope said with a straight face. "What are you going to tell them?"

"Turtledoves mate for life," he said, eyes twinkling. "Even glass ones."

She nodded sagely. "*Turr, turr.*"

"Speech!" the crowd shouted.

"I love you," Nicholas murmured into her ear.

"I love you, too," she whispered back and looped her arm through his.

They exchanged a mischievous grin and climbed upon the dais to make their speech together.

THE END

Now that Saint Nick is off the market, Christopher is ready to find a bride. But when the matchmaker he hires turns out to be the same woman he had a public spat with the day before, nothing goes as planned!

Join the fun in *Wish Upon a Duke*, the next romance in the *12 Dukes of Christmas* series!

Keep turning for a **Sneak Peek**!

AUTHOR'S NOTE

I hope you had as much fun reading about Penelope and Nicholas as I did writing them! Their story came to me from very diverse ideas.

One day, I was shaking my head about the over-the-top "You'll need to hide from all the women!" advertisements of men's colognes, similar to *Hai Karate* and *Axe Body Spray*.

I began to wonder what the Regency equivalent might look like, and asked myself: What if the creator is a woman, rather than a man? What if her ultimate goal is to give the power to women? And what if her love interest is a dashing London rake who hates her perfume because it cramps his style?

(In case it's not obvious, I spend a good chunk of my work day giggling at my keyboard.)

"Saint Nick" is more directly related to Christmas. Not only is his name a synonym for Santa Claus, many of his quirks and actions are inspired by Christmas stories and carols.

He visits only one night, he spends all his time in his workshop, he always brings a gift, he can't resist the cookies left for him on the mantel, he goes up on the housetop, and many more.

Plus, there's Penelope's prediction that he'll one day be a fat man with white hair sitting around eating cookies!

Poor, long-suffering Nicholas. If it makes him feel better, *I* like to think of him as Hot Santa. Which means that Penelope—baker of cookies and lover of workshops—is destined to become his Mrs. Claus, apron and all.

Thank you for joining me on their journey to love. No matter what time of year you read this romance, I hope it brings you moments of good cheer!

xoxo,

Erica Ridley

ACKNOWLEDGMENTS

As always, I could not have written this book without the invaluable support of my critique partner and copy editors. Huge thanks go out to Erica Monroe, Summer Warren, and April Bennett. You are the best!

Lastly, I want to thank the *12 Dukes of Christmas* facebook group, my *Historical Romance Book Club,* and my fabulous street team. Your enthusiasm makes the romance happen.

Thank you so much!

WISH UPON A DUKE

Love, actually...

Rumor has it, charming adventurer Christopher Pringle is finally ready to settle down. He's searching for a free-spirited bride to join him on his travels. But when the matchmaker he hires turns out to be the woman he had a public spat with the day before, nothing goes as planned!

Miss Gloria Godwin loves exploring the world... from the safety of a book. She detests her dashing client's attempts to force her from her comfort zone. It should be easy to marry off the handsome heir to a dukedom. But the more she tries to match him to other women, the harder it gets to say goodbye.

Gloria's heart pounded with pleasure.

Christopher was bending a rule, just for her. He wasn't merely allowing her to be herself, no matter how silly that might be, but actively joining his imagination with hers.

She'd like to join a few more bits together.

He was temptation incarnate. Everything about him with something she shouldn't have or couldn't have, but wanted very much. She sank her fingers into his hair as she kissed him.

His lips were firm and generous, his tongue hot and demanding. She would relinquish anything he wanted if he would give her everything she needed. Her body yearned for him, from her banging heart to the rush of desire racing through her blood. She might lose him on the morrow, but she would not allow tonight to pass them by.

"Tell me about your travels," she murmured

between kisses. "Do all cultures require cravats?"

He murmured *No* without separating his mouth from hers.

She slid her fingers from his hair down to his neckcloth. In moments, she untied the knot. With a flourish, she tossed the soft square of white silk aside.

"Tourists," she murmured. "Always with the neckcloths. Tell me about this very interesting coat of black superfine." She ran her hands over his hard muscles. "Do men in all places hide their gorgeous arms in such things?"

"They do not," he said between kisses. "Horrid custom."

She wriggled her skirts up so that she could better straddle his thighs, then pulled him upright in order to divest him of his coat. When she'd dreamed of what it might be like to undress him, she hadn't realized her fingers would fumble with each button because her hands trembled so. Or that removing each layer of clothing would feel like stripping away another shield from her heart.

When the well-tailored superfine and accompanying waistcoat joined the forgotten neckcloth outside the blanket, he moved to lay back down.

She stopped him.

"This linen shirt," she said as she ran a fingertip along his shoulder. "It offends my sensibilities."

"A thousand apologies, madam." He crossed his arms at his waistline and removed his shirt in a single fluid movement.

Her breath caught. Having him to command was headier than any brandy. Seeing his naked flesh with her eyes, feeling his strong thighs trapped beneath hers, made her feel more powerful than any star in the sky. He wasn't looking at his telescope. He was looking at her. Submitting to her every wish because his desire matched her own.

His hot gaze never wavered from hers. "How else may I be of service?"

THANK YOU FOR READING

Love talking books with fellow readers?

Join the *Historical Romance Book Club* for prizes, books, and live chats with your favorite romance authors:
Facebook.com/groups/HistRomBookClub

Check out the *12 Dukes of Christmas* facebook group for giveaways and exclusive content:
Facebook.com/groups/DukesOfChristmas

Join the *Rogues to Riches* facebook group for insider info and first looks at future books in the series:
Facebook.com/groups/RoguesToRiches

Check out the *Dukes of War* facebook group for giveaways and exclusive content:
Facebook.com/groups/DukesOfWar

And check out the official website for sneak peeks and more:

www.EricaRidley.com/books

In order, the 12 Dukes of Christmas:

Once Upon a Duke
Kiss of a Duke
Wish Upon a Duke
Never Say Duke
Dukes, Actually
The Duke's Bride
The Duke's Embrace
The Duke's Desire
Dawn With a Duke
One Night With a Duke
Ten Days With a Duke
Forever Your Duke

In order, the Rogues to Riches books are:

Lord of Chance
Lord of Pleasure
Lord of Night
Lord of Temptation
Lord of Secrets
Lord of Vice

In order, the Dukes of War books are:

The Viscount's Tempting Minx (FREE!)
The Earl's Defiant Wallflower
The Captain's Bluestocking Mistress
The Major's Faux Fiancée
The Brigadier's Runaway Bride

The Pirate's Tempting Stowaway
The Duke's Accidental Wife

Want to be the first to know about new releases?

Sign up at http://ridley.vip for members-only exclusives, including advance notice of pre-orders, as well as contests, giveaways, freebies, and 99¢ deals!

You can also follow me on Bookbub.

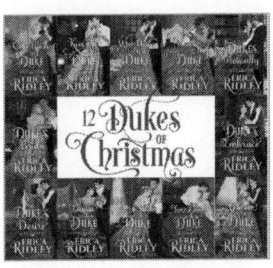

THANK YOU FOR READING

ABOUT THE AUTHOR

Erica Ridley is a *New York Times* and *USA Today* best-selling author of historical romance novels.

In the new *Rogues to Riches* historical romance series, Cinderella stories aren't just for princesses... Sigh-worthy Regency rogues sweep strong-willed young ladies into whirlwind rags-to-riches romance with rollicking adventure.

The popular *Dukes of War* series features roguish peers and dashing war heroes who return from battle only to be thrust into the splendor and madness of Regency England.

When not reading or writing romances, Erica can be found riding camels in Africa, ziplining through rainforests in Central America, or getting hopelessly lost in the middle of Budapest.

~

Let's be friends! Find Erica on:
www.EricaRidley.com

Printed in Germany
by Amazon Distribution
GmbH, Leipzig